Fifth
Grade
Fever

FIFTH GRADE FEVER

Michele Granger

Dutton Children's Books

NEW YORK

Library of Congress Cataloging-in-Publication Data

Granger, Michele.
Fifth grade fever / by Michele Granger.—1st ed.
p. cm.
Summary: Marty and her best friend Nina have a fight,
wear M&M lipstick, and even do their homework in order
to impress their handsome new fifth grade teacher.
ISBN 0-525-45279-6
[1. Schools—Fiction. 2. Teachers—Fiction.] I. Title.
PZ7.G76619Fi 1995 [Fic]—dc20 94-31893 CIP AC

Published in the United States by Dutton Children's Books,
a division of Penguin Books USA Inc.
375 Hudson Street, New York, New York 10014

Designed by Amy Berniker
Printed in USA
First Edition
3 5 7 9 8 6 4 2

For Bob, with love

Fifth
Grade
Fever

C H A P T E R

One

It was Tuesday, the very last day of summer vacation, when the postcard with Marty's fifth grade class assignment finally came in the mail. She tore to the kitchen phone the minute she read it and dialed her best friend, Nina's, number.

Nina answered on the second ring. "Hello."

"It's me," Marty said. "I got a guy. He must be the new teacher."

"Me, too!" Nina shouted. "Mr. *Truesdale!* Don't you love that name?"

"Yeah," Marty said. "I hope he's cute." She pushed her bangs from her forehead and smoothed her T-shirt. Somehow she'd have to look better by tomorrow. A *lot* better.

"No way," said Nina. "Someone cute would never be teaching fifth grade."

"Why not? With a name like Truesdale, he's got to be." Marty had never known a real person with such a movie-star-sounding name.

"A cute guy would be doing something else," said Nina, "like being a lifeguard or making Coke commercials."

Marty shifted the phone to her other ear. "We are *so* lucky. Boy, am I glad we didn't get that horrible Mrs. Luciano."

"*So* glad!" Nina agreed.

"I hope we get to sit together," Marty said. "Maybe he'll do it alphabetically."

"Yeah," said Nina. "Guardino and then Gordon. You'd be right behind me."

"In *front* of you, you mean," Marty said. "Don't you know the alphabet yet?" Marty might not be a brain, but at least she knew that much.

"Whatever . . ." Nina said. "Let's go over to school right now. Maybe we'll see him."

"But what if he sees *us?*" Marty asked. She wasn't as much of a daredevil as Nina was. She wasn't a daredevil at *all*.

"*So?*"

"Well . . . okay," Marty said. It usually didn't take much for Nina to talk her into things.

"Meet you there," said Nina. "I'm leaving this minute."

"Me, too." Marty hung up.

"Going to Nina's!" she hollered up the stairs to her

mother. She didn't want to explain why they were going to the school. Then she ran for the back door.

Whenever anyone in the Gordon house ran, their dog, Pooh-bah, seemed to think that something exciting was happening. Marty nearly tripped over him as he leaped around her, barking like crazy.

"Down, Pooh!" Marty tried to push him away, but it wasn't easy to do. He was enormous—a black poodle, almost as tall as Marty when he stood on his hind legs.

Marty's mother yelled something back to her. Marty couldn't quite make it out over the dog's barking, but it didn't sound like "no," so she kept going. Pooh ran ahead.

Marty stopped to grab an apple from the basket on the kitchen table. Her little brother, Robbie, was there, reading a huge book. Pooh-bah yipped and bumped the underside of Robbie's book with his nose. But Robbie ignored him.

"Martha," he said, without looking up, "did you know that the Mexican free-tailed bats in Texas eat over six thousand, six hundred tons of insects per year?"

Marty pushed past him. "I didn't know. I don't *want* to know. And *don't* call me Martha," she said through a mouthful of apple.

Robbie left his book on the table and followed Marty. "Well, it's your *real* name."

"Hold the dog while I open the door," Marty said. "I'm *not* taking him."

"But he wants to go." Robbie seemed to notice Pooh for the first time.

"Got him?" Marty hollered over the dog's commotion.

Robbie nodded. He clutched Pooh-bah's collar with two hands and stood with his feet braced.

Marty patted Robbie's head. "Thanks, Roberto Philipo Gordono."

She slipped out. The door banged behind her.

"It's Robert Philip Gordon, Martha!" Robbie yelled through the screen. "And you know it!"

Marty headed down the walk.

Oh, why couldn't she have a regular little brother? One who played baseball or something? Instead, she had an eight-year-old one who was too smart for his own good and absolutely obsessed with bats. When he wasn't reading about them, he was trying to tell someone about them. And a lot of the time, the person he was trying to tell was *her*.

"Mar-te-e-e!" It was Nina. She ran toward Marty with her black curls flying. Nina had wild hair that went in every direction no matter how much she tried to tame it with all the barrettes and headbands her mother was always buying for her.

Nina was out of breath. "What took you so long?"

"I walked as fast as I could." Marty took another bite of her apple.

"Let's look in the teachers' parking lot first," Nina said as they headed up the hill toward the school. "See if we can spot his car."

At the parking lot gate, they looked down the line of cars. There was Mrs. Luciano's old black bomber and all the

6

rest that Marty remembered from last year. But there was one on the end that she didn't recognize.

"That must be his." Marty pointed to a tan VW.

"Let's go check it out," Nina said.

"What if someone sees us?" Marty whispered.

Nina gave Marty's arm a little punch. "*C'mon!*" She crouched low and scuttled among the other teachers' cars.

Marty hesitated for a second. Then she followed Nina. When they reached the VW, she looked in the windows on one side, while Nina looked in on the other side. It wasn't very satisfying, though. There was only a folded-up newspaper on the front seat and a couple of soda cans on the floor in the back.

"Aha!" Nina said. "Diet soda. You know what *that* means."

Marty didn't. But she didn't want to say so. She waited, hoping that Nina would go on.

"He's got a girlfriend," Nina announced.

"How do you know?"

They'd forgotten to keep whispering.

" 'Cause guys never drink diet soda," said Nina.

"They do if they're fat."

"Oh, gross!" Nina groaned. "I knew it. I just knew it. We finally get a guy teacher and he turns out to be a blimp."

Marty leaned in despair against the VW. Nina leaned next to her.

A voice startled Marty. "What are you two doing here?"

It was Beverly Bridges. Beverly was all dressed up, as if school had already started. She wore a plaid pleated skirt and a clean white blouse, neatly tucked in. On her feet were white socks, folded down perfectly, and white sneakers without a speck of dirt on them. Beverly was the sort of girl who asked permission to stay in at recess to wash the chalkboards. And she was always doing something for extra credit.

In their school, there were two classes of each grade, but Beverly Bridges had been in Marty's room every year since kindergarten. Just once, Marty wanted to be spared. One year without Beverly Bridges. One. Just one.

And let it be this one. Marty offered a silent prayer.

"Who'd you get?" Nina asked Beverly.

"Mr. Truesdale," Beverly said. "He's new."

In her heart, Marty groaned. "We know," she said. "We got him, too."

"He's *very* nice," Beverly said. "My mother and I were just in talking to him. She's president of the PTA this year, you know. We came to welcome him. It's his very first year teaching."

Marty was dying to ask Beverly if Mr. Truesdale was cute. But Beverly wouldn't understand the importance of such a thing. Or if she did, she wouldn't admit it.

"We brought him a plant," Beverly went on.

Nina, who always came out with whatever popped into her mind, said, "Hey, Beverly, is he fat?"

"Mr. Truesdale?" Beverly sounded shocked.

Nina cocked her thumb at the VW. "Yeah. He's got diet soda cans on his car floor."

Beverly raised her eyebrows and rose up on her toes a

little, but she didn't look in the car. "Snoops!" she said. "Of course he's not fat. He's quite handsome."

Under her breath to Marty, Nina said, "Girlfriend theory confirmed."

"What did you say?" Beverly asked.

"Bever-le-e-e!" It was Mrs. Bridges. She stood on the school steps, clutching her purse in front of her in both hands.

"Coming!" Beverly ran off toward her mother. Coming as soon as she was called was another thing that Beverly always did. "See you in class!" she yelled back over her shoulder.

Marty waved. But Nina turned her back on Beverly and stuck a finger down her throat. She pretended to gag. Then she said in a singsong voice, " 'He's quite handsome.' "

" 'We just came to welcome him,' " Marty answered in the same kind of voice.

"Can I help you girls with anything?"

A guy in a plaid shirt and chino pants was walking toward the VW. A *gorgeous* guy.

Marty straightened up. She ran her hand over the fender, polishing the place where she'd been leaning.

"Uh, no," Marty stammered. "We were—uh—just—uh . . ."

"Resting," Nina finished.

Marty caught herself polishing the fender and pulled her hand away. "Yes—resting," she agreed. It *must* be him. It *had* to be Mr. Truesdale.

"Better do it now," he said. "Come tomorrow, the resting will all be over."

He was smiling. He was tanned. Maybe Nina had been right about the lifeguard stuff.

Marty gave a nervous little laugh and glanced quickly at her sneakers—grungy old ones with the laces gone. Had they ever been as white as Beverly's?

"Well, if you'll excuse me . . ." The guy jingled his car keys.

"Oh, sorry." Marty leaped away from the car. She forced herself to look at his eyes. They were blue, blue, bluer than any eyes she'd ever seen.

"Anyway . . ." Nina edged away. "We were just going."

"Just going," Marty repeated, sounding like Nina's parrot. It took all her willpower not to run away.

"Enjoy your rest," the guy-who-must-be-Mr. Truesdale said.

Then he got into the VW and pulled away. Marty watched as the car went out of the parking lot and down the street. Finally, it disappeared around a corner.

"Oh, *Marty!*" Nina said.

"Do you think it's really him?" Marty asked. "What if it isn't?" Maybe a guy that gorgeous *wouldn't* teach fifth grade.

"Of *course* it's him," said Nina. "We lucked out, Mart. For once, we really lucked out."

"Except for Beverly," Marty reminded her. She could already picture Beverly clapping the erasers together.

"Oh, yeah." Nina rolled her eyes. "*Beverly.*"

"I mean, *she* brought him a plant," said Marty. "And he's already caught *us* spying on him."

"She just wants to be the teacher's pet," Nina said.

"Like she *always* is," said Marty.

"Not this year." Nina started walking.

Marty fell into step beside her. "Tell Beverly that."

"I don't have to," Nina said. "She'll see for herself. This year's teacher's pets are going to be—" She stopped walking. She swept her arm wide and said in an announcer-sounding voice, "Nina Guardino and Marty Gordon!"

"How are we going to do that?" Marty asked.

"Easy," Nina said. "We're charming and smart and beautiful, aren't we?"

"Well . . ." Marty looked down at her ratty sneakers. She remembered Nina's alphabet mistake.

"Just say yes," Nina said.

"Yes." Marty smiled at Nina. But still she wondered— how *are* we going to do it?

Two

————— ✳ —————

Marty's first-day-of-school clothes were all wrong. And this was the third outfit she'd put on. The other ones had been even worse. She'd thought she looked okay in the mirror upstairs. But now, it seemed that the hem of her skirt dipped down longer on one side. And whenever she raised her arms, the tail of her blouse popped out from beneath her waistband. She'd have to remember to keep her arms down.

"And my *hair!*" Marty stared miserably in the hall mirror.

Her bangs had been growing in for what seemed like forever. But they still weren't long enough to tuck behind her ear, and they wouldn't stay pushed to the side, either.

"Why don't you just clip them over, like this, with one

of your nice barrettes?" Marty's mother held the bangs off her face.

"Ma!" Marty snatched her mother's hand away.

"Just a suggestion." Her mother went back to the kitchen.

"Gravity's against you," Robbie observed from his post by the front door.

He had been all ready to go since before their father had left for work. Now he was waiting for the van to pick him up and take him to his special school for gifted children. "You can't deny a force like gravity just because you're growing your bangs out."

"Shut up, Robbie," Marty said. "Ma, will you tell Robbie to shut up?"

"Robbie," their mother called from the kitchen, "don't bother your sister. She's having a hair crisis."

"I am *not!*"

"It's not nice to lie, *Mar-tha*," Robbie said.

"Robbie . . ." their mother called again.

Marty started toward him. "How would you like to have a fat lip for the first day of school?"

"Hello! Hello!" Nina came in the back door. "It's me!"

"Nina!" Marty said. "What are you doing here?"

Pooh-bah went crazy. He leaped on Nina, licking her face all over.

"Hey, Pooh!" Nina pushed him down and wiped her face. "I couldn't wait another minute. I had to come over."

"My hair won't stay back." Marty pushed at her bangs

again. But as soon as she took her hand away, they flopped over one eye.

Nina fluffed Marty's bangs with her fingers. "There. They're fine. Just don't move your head too much. Now, let's go."

Nina's own hair was in its usual out-of-control state, which didn't seem to worry her at all.

A horn sounded.

"They're here!" Robbie grabbed his backpack and ran out the door, sending Pooh into another barking frenzy.

Marty's mother ran out of the kitchen, shouting over the dog's noise, "Good-bye, darling! Have a great day!"

She needn't have bothered to say it. Robbie *always* had a great day at school. Marty's school days, however, were usually another matter.

But not this year, Marty reminded herself, trying to get her courage up. She sneaked another look at her hair in the hall mirror. Still a disaster.

"Will you come *on?*" Nina grabbed Marty's arm. "Really, you look great."

Nina hustled Marty toward the back door.

"Good-bye, girls!" Mrs. Gordon called.

They started off toward school.

Nina pulled one of her boingy curls and let it spring back. "I could hardly sleep last night," she said. "I was so excited."

"Me, too," said Marty. "But it wasn't like the Christmas-is-coming kind of excited. It was more like the going-to-the-dentist kind of excited."

"Oh, Mart. *Why?* This is going to be terrific."

"Well . . ." Marty hesitated. "I was wondering. Do you have some kind of a . . . plan?"

"Plan?"

"Yeah," Marty said. "A plan for how we can get to be Mr. Truesdale's pets. I mean, I've never been a teacher's pet before and neither have you."

They walked by the teachers' parking lot. The VW was there.

"There's always a first time," Nina said.

Marty wished she could feel as sure as Nina did. Nina was wearing her usual jeans, T-shirt, and sneakers, just as if it were any other day. Marty guessed that *looking* like a teacher's pet wasn't part of the deal—as far as Nina was concerned.

"Yeah. But you-know-who has a lot of experience at it," Marty reminded her. "She's a pro." She thought of Beverly's perfect sneakers.

"Well . . ." Nina adjusted her headband. "For one thing, we'll get great grades. All A's."

"Nina, you've never gotten an A in your entire life," Marty said. "Not one!"

"I was just fooling around before." Nina pulled a poker face. "This year I'm a serious student."

Marty laughed. "We'll do all our homework," she said.

"Every night," Nina agreed. "*And* we'll remember to turn it in."

"We won't pass notes to each other," said Marty.

"Never," Nina said. "And we won't talk unless we're called on."

"We'll sit in the front row and pay attention to everything he says." Marty could just picture it.

Nina's hand shot up in the air. "We'll raise our hand when we know the answer."

"And we'll *always* know the answer!" Marty shouted.

"Yes!"

They jumped up and slapped hands in the air, a high five. Marty's blouse pulled completely out of her skirt.

"We'll bring him presents." Marty jammed her shirttail back under her waistband as she walked. "Apples and stuff."

"And we'll say his name a lot," Nina said. " 'Yes, Mr. Truesdale. No, Mr. Truesdale.' Teachers love it when you do that."

"Or 'sir'!" Marty said. "Sir's even better."

Nina pulled at the sides of her jeans, as if she were wearing a skirt, and curtsied. "Sir, may I please be excused?"

They both giggled.

"We'll wash the chalkboards," Marty said.

"And clap the erasers," Nina added.

"We'll tie our book report covers together with beautiful ribbons." Marty felt full of wonderful ideas.

"We'll make stuff out of papier-mâché for extra credit," said Nina.

Marty paused. "That's not *too* kiss-uppy, is it?" Extra credit was Beverly's middle name.

Nina looked like she was thinking. Then she said, "Nah! *You* think so?"

"Nah!" Marty said. Maybe you had to kiss up a little to be a teacher's pet.

They went through the open gate into the school yard. Marty stopped to pull up her socks. The elastic in them was going and they had slipped down into her sneakers. She tucked in her blouse and yanked at her hem. She knew she probably still looked terrible, but she felt a little better than she had before. After all, now they had a plan. A really good plan.

The school yard was crowded with kids. Marty looked around for Beverly, but she didn't see her.

The fifth graders were all buzzing about the new teacher. Would he be nice or a screamer? Would he give a lot of homework? Everyone was dying to know. But they all agreed that no matter how Mr. Truesdale turned out, he had to be better than Mrs. Luciano. The poor kids in her class *knew* what they were getting, and it wasn't good.

"Don't tell anyone," Nina said, "about our plan."

Marty pressed her lips together and drew her fingers across them as if she were closing a zipper.

As they got closer to the big red double doors, the bell rang. Beverly hadn't shown up yet.

They all shuffled into the building. The two fifth grades were off on a corridor by themselves, rooms 106 and 107. As she walked toward the fifth grade hall, Marty looked around at the other fifth graders. They were all kids who had been in her class last year or the year before or the year before that. No surprises. There was Frank Fama, who'd worn glasses so long that when he took them off, he looked like a completely different person. David DeVoe, never called Dave, who was an absolute brain in math—Marty's worst subject. Maureen O'Donovan, who'd started wearing a bra last year in *fourth grade*. She always walked with her shoulders hunched up, as if she could hide her grown-up chest that way. Nina had said that she'd have died if it had happened to her, and Marty felt the same way. There was Bernice McCorkle, who was so afraid of dogs that the one time she'd been at Marty's house, they'd had to keep Pooh locked up in the basement the whole time. And then there were all the rest.

Marty scanned the crowd again. "I still don't see her."

"Beverly's around somewhere," Nina said. "No way she'd miss the first day."

"Over to the right, children. Single file. I'm sure you haven't forgotten the rules over the summer." It was Mrs. Luciano. Her voice boomed. She waved her hands with their long red Dragon Lady fingernails.

"Just think," Marty whispered, "we could have gotten *her*."

Nina shuddered.

Marty walked backward, still searching. "I can't believe she's not here."

"Face front and no talking, young lady." Mrs. Luciano didn't miss a thing.

"We lucked out again," Nina said. "Beverly's starting off on the wrong foot. Absent the first day."

"Or late," Marty whispered, trying not to move her lips too much. Mrs. Luciano was behind her now, but Marty didn't take chances the way that Nina did. "Late would be even better."

Nina didn't whisper. She was used to being yelled at by teachers. "We, on the other hand, are definitely on time." She held the swinging door until Marty caught it with her hip.

Marty came through the door sideways and let it swing behind her. Part of her still worried about how she, Marty Gordon, a person who couldn't keep her sneakers clean or grow her bangs out right and who found math almost impossible, was ever going to become the teacher's pet—especially with a teacher as cute as Mr. Truesdale. And how Nina, who'd barely made it out of fourth grade, would do the same.

They stopped outside room 107. Their new room. *His* room. Everyone else was going in. But Nina and Marty stalled until they were the last ones in the hallway.

"We'll make a more dramatic entrance this way," Nina said.

When everyone else had gone inside, Marty said, "Okay, let's go."

Nina gave Marty the thumbs-up sign.

Marty gave it back.

They started through the doorway.

Then Nina grabbed Marty's arm and pulled her back into the hall. "Wait. Quick, smell my face."

"What?"

"Do I smell like dog spit?" Nina asked. "Pooh slobbered all over me."

Marty glanced around. The hall was empty. She gave Nina's face a quick but thorough sniff. "You're okay."

Nina rubbed her cheeks. "Thanks."

Then they went into the classroom. Most of the kids were already in their seats. They were all talking. But the sound was more hum than words.

Mr. Truesdale stood by his desk at the front of the room. It was him. The VW guy from yesterday. Even more gorgeous than Marty remembered. He was wearing chino pants again. Only today, instead of the plaid shirt, he wore a white one that looked great with his tan. He had on a dark blue sports jacket, too, and a red tie with teeny dots on it. He looked like someone in a magazine.

"Well . . ." He flashed a gleaming, straight row of teeth. "Are you two all rested up?"

He *remembered* them. He was smiling at them. He must like them already.

Marty's laugh sounded more like a bark. She pulled at her bangs.

"Oh . . . yeah." Nina smiled right back at him. Then

she moved toward the desks. "Can we just sit anywhere?"

"For now," Mr. Truesdale said. "Yes. Sit anywhere."

All the front-row seats were taken, except for one that had a backpack on it, staking it out for somebody.

Nina and Marty slid into seats next to each other. They were near the back, but at least it wasn't the very last row.

Then Marty saw Beverly. She was over by the windows, watering the plants on the sill.

"Look," Marty whispered to Nina. *"Beverly."*

Beverly must have heard her. She looked up and caught Marty staring. Beverly smiled and wiggled her fingers in a little wave. Then she went back to her watering.

"She must have come in early," Nina whispered.

Marty looked down the row of pots on the windowsill. "Do you think she brought him *all* those plants?"

"Who cares?" Nina flipped through her notebook. "We've got a great plan, Mart. This is going to be a piece of cake."

"A piece of cake," Marty repeated. But she didn't really believe it.

Then Beverly finished her watering and walked over to the desk with the backpack on it. She lifted it off and took her seat. Right in front of Mr. Truesdale's desk.

Three

It was almost time for lunch, and Mr. Truesdale still hadn't changed them from the seats that they'd picked that morning. At first it hadn't seemed that bad. But now Marty was starting to hate being in the back. She was sure that Beverly was smiling at Mr. Truesdale every chance she got. Beverly was right there, practically under his nose.

All of Marty's other teachers had put the kids in seats alphabetically or by how tall they were or boy-girl, boy-girl, or some other way. But Mr. Truesdale was new. Maybe he didn't know how to do that. He didn't know some other stuff, either. Like how to talk like a teacher. He didn't use that do-this-or-die voice. And, so far, he hadn't given anyone the Mean Teacher Stare. He just talked to them regular, as if they were real people instead of the kids in his class. He smiled a lot. It was weird. It was wonderful.

Marty was bursting to talk to Nina. Neither of them had said a word to each other since they'd stopped whispering when the nine o'clock bell had rung. They hadn't passed one note. They had barely even looked at one another. Trying to be the teacher's pet was *so* hard. How did Beverly do it *every* day, year after year? But maybe it wasn't so hard for her. She didn't have anyone to talk to anyway. Who'd want to talk to *her?*

Marty sat forward in her seat. She opened her eyes wide in a look of complete attention, even though Mr. Truesdale was only telling them how to do their book reports. Marty loved the way he leaned against the desk as he talked. He looked so cool. So handsome. And he was *her* teacher.

Marty's face started to ache from wearing its completely-paying-attention look so long. But she was afraid to change it. Not that Mr. Truesdale cared. How could he? He couldn't even *see* her, stuck behind David DeVoe's big, brainy head the way she was. Maybe if she moved her seat over a little, Mr. Truesdale would notice her.

Marty gripped the sides of her chair and jumped it sideways. But it was the kind of seat that had the desk attached to it and the whole thing came with her. Beverly turned to stare. But Mr. Truesdale mustn't have heard. He went right on talking.

"*P-s-s-st!*" It was Nina. She motioned wildly with her

hands for Marty to move back. Nina looked panicked, as if Marty had just done something terrible. As if she'd blown their whole plan.

Marty scooted her chair back. It made an awful scraping sound. This time, *everyone* turned to stare. Why had she listened to Nina?

Mr. Truesdale raised his perfect eyebrows. "Having some trouble back there?" he asked.

Marty licked her lips. Her tongue felt too big for her mouth. "Uh—no . . ." she managed to say.

"Good," Mr. Truesdale said.

Marty glanced over at Nina. But Nina's face was hidden in her hands.

Then Mr. Truesdale told them that they'd have a book report due every two weeks, which seemed like an awful lot of book reports.

At last, the lunch bell rang. All the kids put their stuff away and started moving toward the coatroom for their backpacks.

Mr. Truesdale didn't stop them. He just said, "We'll pick up here after lunch," raising his voice a little to be heard over the commotion.

He wasn't going to be one of those remain-in-your-seats-until-I-dismiss-you kind of teachers. Boy, were *they* lucky!

As soon as they were out in the hall, Nina grabbed Marty's arm. "I can't believe you did that!" she said.

"I had to," said Marty. "He can't see me at all where I'm sitting. Big Brain DeVoe's blocking me."

Nina hurried down the stairs to the lunchroom with Marty close behind her. "Well, I'm back there, too." Nina talked over her shoulder. "And we're being so good. It's such a waste."

They pushed through the swinging doors. Marty smelled that yucky school lunch smell—boiled hot dogs and who knew what else. She was so glad she'd brought her lunch from home. Actually, she and Nina never bought the school lunch except on the Fridays when they had pizza.

Marty and Nina slid into seats across the table from each other. They sat at the end of the table, away from everyone else, so they could talk.

"This stinks," Nina said. She was unwrapping her sandwich.

"What did your mother give you?" Marty asked. She had her favorite—tuna on whole wheat.

"Not my *sandwich*," Nina said. "It's fine. Salami and mayo, like always." She took a bite. Still chewing, she said, "Our seats. That's what stinks. We've got to move them."

"At least Mr. Truesdale can see you," Marty said. "He doesn't know I exist."

"We'll never get in good with him as long as we're stuck in the back," said Nina.

"And Beverly's in the front." Marty polished her apple on her sleeve.

Nina crumpled the waxed paper from her sandwich into a ball, took aim, and tossed it into the trash barrel. "Perfect shot," she said. "Two points."

"So what are we going to do?" Marty asked. She wondered if teacher's pets were supposed to throw out their lunch trash the way Nina just had.

Nina was busy getting out her cookies. "We'll think of something," she said.

Frank Fama came up to their table, carrying a school lunch tray full of food. The lunch period was almost over. He must have been about the last one in line. "Can I sit here?" he asked.

Nina and Marty exchanged looks.

Marty didn't really want anyone else sitting near them, but it seemed mean to say no, especially since they were almost finished. "Go ahead," she said.

"Thanks." Frank put his tray on the table next to Marty and sat down.

The lunch was even more disgusting close up. The hot dog had a big split in it and the roll wasn't toasted. There were peas and carrots in a little pile and fruit cocktail in a white paper cup.

"I'd drink the milk and forget the rest if I were you," Nina told Frank.

"It's not too bad." Frank picked up his hot dog and took a bite. "How do you like Truesdale?" His mouth was full of hot dog.

"Oh, he's all right, I guess." Nina pressed her fingertip into her cookie crumbs and licked them off. She was doing a perfect imitation of someone who didn't care.

"He's okay," Marty said.

If Frank could tell how they *really* felt about Mr. Truesdale, he gave no sign.

"Yeah." Frank dug into his fruit cocktail. "He kind of lets the class go wild, but he seems like a pretty good guy."

Marty wanted to defend Mr. Truesdale, but she just shrugged. She was afraid she might blush if she said his name out loud.

Frank kept eating. Finally he sucked up the last of his milk through his straw with a loud noise. Then he took off his glasses and started polishing them with his school lunch napkin. He had that raccoony look he always had without his glasses.

He was getting ready to put them on again, when Nina's hand shot out. "Can I try them?" she asked.

"Well . . ." Frank hesitated. "I guess so. But be careful."

Marty wasn't the only one who had a hard time saying no to Nina.

Nina hooked a bow over each ear. "Wow! How can you see with these things?"

"I can't see too much without them." Frank already had his hand out to reclaim the glasses.

Nina ignored him. "Wow," she said again. "Marty, you try them." She pulled off the glasses and handed them to Marty.

Marty looked at Frank to see if it was okay. But he only shrugged. She put the glasses on.

"You're all blurry," Marty said.

"Okay," said Frank. "The fun's over. Give them back."

Marty gave Frank his glasses just as the bell rang for the end of lunch. Frank grabbed them and hurried away.

"We didn't even get to go outside," Marty said.

"No." Nina gathered up the rest of her lunch trash. "But Frank's glasses just gave me a great idea."

"What?"

Nina grabbed Marty's elbow and whispered in her ear. "I know how we can get to move up front."

"How?"

"I'll say I can't see from where I am," Nina said. "That I need glasses but they haven't come in yet."

"And what'll *I* say?" Marty asked. "It can't be the same thing."

"No." Nina seemed to be thinking as she walked. Suddenly she stopped short. "I know!" she said. "You'll say you can't hear."

"But I don't have a hearing aid or anything."

"You don't need one," Nina said. "It's not that bad"—she lowered her voice—"*yet.*"

"But that's a lie," Marty said. "We'll never get away with it." And besides, Marty thought, I want him to think that I'm perfect in every way.

"He's new. He doesn't know any better," said Nina. "And you have to ask yourself, Is it a lie for a good reason or a bad reason?"

Marty considered. "Good," she finally answered.

"There. See?" Nina said. "We'll do it first chance we get."

But it seemed that their chance would never come.

Right after lunch they went to art. When they came back, they had to read a chapter for social studies and answer the questions at the end. Mr. Truesdale never did get back to talking about all those book reports they were going to have to do.

Marty *could* have raised her hand to say that she couldn't hear Mr. Truesdale's directions. But, somehow, she just couldn't make herself do it. If only Nina would go first. Maybe that would give her the nerve. Whenever Mr. Truesdale talked, Marty leaned forward in her seat and cupped her hand around her left ear (that was the one with the problem, she'd decided). But he didn't seem to notice.

Then Mr. Truesdale began to put some math problems on the board. "This is just a little test," he announced, "to see what you've remembered over the summer."

Just the sight of numbers made Marty's stomach go tight. Now he'd know what a dummy she was.

But Nina didn't look worried, though she was every bit as bad at math as Marty was—maybe even worse. Nina gave Marty a knowing look and raised her hand.

Mr. Truesdale was busy writing the problems on the board. Nina kept her hand in the air. She was probably afraid she'd lose her courage if she took it down. He didn't notice Nina's waving till he'd finished and turned to look at the class.

"Yes . . . uh . . ." He couldn't seem to remember Nina's name.

"Nina," Nina finished for him. "Nina Guardino. Could I please speak to you privately, sir?"

She was calling him "sir," just as they'd said they would.

"Of course," Mr. Truesdale said. "Come right out in the hall!"

Nina went out with Mr. Truesdale. Everyone was whispering.

"What's the matter with her?" Frank asked Marty.

Marty shrugged and studied her desktop. She squirmed in her seat, as jittery as if she were the one out there in the hall.

Then they came back in. Nina followed Mr. Truesdale to the front of the room. She stood at his side, squinting. He looked over the kids in the front row. Nina didn't look at Marty.

Finally he said, "Ms. Bridges, you've been *so* cooperative. I wonder if you'd mind trading seats with Ms. Guardino. It seems she's having trouble seeing the board."

"Uh . . ." Beverly hesitated. "No. Of course not, Mr. Truesdale. I'd be happy to help." She sounded anything but happy.

Beverly turned to glare at Marty. Then she pulled out her books and stacked them in a pile.

Nina came back to her old desk, still squinting. She didn't

say a word to Marty as she got out all her things. But on her way back up the aisle, she gave the leg of Marty's chair a kick.

Then Beverly marched down the aisle and took her new seat—right next to Marty.

Four

Marty picked at the broccoli on her dinner plate. She couldn't stop thinking about their plan to be Mr. Truesdale's pets and how it was never going to work as long as she was such a chicken.

Her father tapped her arm. "Marty, sit up and eat your dinner. You look like you're in another world."

She was. The world where she would be sitting next to Beverly Bridges *forever*.

"Where do *you* think we should put it, Marth?" Robbie asked.

"What?"

"The bat house," Robbie said.

"*What* bat house?" Marty asked.

"The one Dad and I are building for my independent study project at school." Robbie held out a book to Marty. "See? The plans are right in here."

Marty waved the book away. "Can't you see I'm eating?"

"If you can call it that," her mother said.

"It says that a single house can be occupied by a hundred or more bats," Robbie read. He looked up. "But a finished house is only twenty-seven by nine inches, so it could go almost anywhere."

"That's great," said Marty. "More than a hundred bats right in our own yard."

"Rob," their mother said, "why don't you put the book away till we're through with dinner?"

Robbie tore off a shred of his paper napkin and stuck it in the book to keep his place. He took a last peek before he slid the book under his chair.

"I think it's a marvelous project." Their father sawed away at his roast beef. "A wonderful start to what I'm sure will be a very successful school year." Then he looked at Marty. "For *both* of you," he added.

Marty knew that he probably thought she was going to bomb out again. She'd show *him*.

Their mother set down her glass of iced tea. "Well, Marty," she said, "we haven't heard much from you. Tell us about that new teacher of yours."

"Mr. Truesdale?" Marty's heart beat faster just saying his name. "There's not too much to tell. It's just the first day."

She concentrated on pushing the food around on her plate. If she made enough spaces maybe her mother wouldn't notice that she'd hardly eaten a bite.

"So, what's he like?" Mrs. Gordon persisted.

"He's nice," Marty said.

Nice? He was the *best.* But she didn't want to say more. She was rotten at keeping secrets, especially from her mother. If she wasn't careful, she might blurt out the whole thing—about Nina's lie and the one she wished she could tell, too.

"The one thing we have to be sure of," Robbie said, "is that the lumber we get hasn't been treated with any preservatives or insecticides."

Marty stared at him.

"Robbie," their mother said, "I was asking Marty about her teacher."

"That's okay," said Marty. For once, she was grateful to Robbie for interrupting her. She picked up her plate, hoping no one would see how full it still was. "Is everyone done? Can I clear?"

"Well, it could harm the bats," Robbie went on. "Those chemicals aren't good for them."

"We'll be careful, son." His father patted Robbie's arm. "Don't you worry."

"And next time, don't interrupt," Mrs. Gordon told Robbie. She turned to Marty. "Go ahead."

Marty wasn't sure if she meant for her to go ahead and

talk or to go ahead and clear. But she sprang up and started clearing the table. Pooh jumped up when Marty did. Marty whisked the plates off the table and practically ran with them to the sink. She wanted to look too busy to talk. Pooh trailed her, watching the plates with hopeful eyes.

"Correct me if I'm wrong, Marth," Robbie said. "But didn't you clear last night? I think it's your night to get dessert and sweep the floor."

Marty pulled the dishwashing detergent from under the sink and slammed the cabinet door. "Thanks for telling me when I'm almost done."

"But you were so fast," Robbie said.

Ordinarily, Marty would have argued with him, but this time, she knew he was right. "Tell you what," she said, "I'll do it *all* tonight." She squirted dishwashing liquid into the compartment in the washer door and clicked it closed. "Your job *and* my job. How's that?" She would be entirely too busy to discuss anything.

"That's great, Marth," Robbie said, "but won't it mess up the schedule?"

Robbie was crazy about schedules.

"Nah," Marty said. "Tomorrow we'll go back to the old routine. I'll clear like I'm supposed to."

"I guess that'll be okay," Robbie said. But he looked unconvinced.

The phone rang.

"Hello," Mr. Gordon said. "Yes, she is. Just a moment."

He covered the receiver with his hand. "Marty, it's Nina. Shall I say that you'll call her back when your chores are done?"

Marty shot Robbie a pleading look.

"Go ahead, Martha," he said in his best martyr voice. "I'll finish for you."

"I love you, Roberto!" Marty kissed the top of Robbie's head as she ran by. She didn't correct him for calling her Martha. "Hang up when I pick up the extension!" she yelled as she tore up the stairs. Marty snatched up the receiver. "Hello."

"Hi, Mart."

Marty waited until she heard the click of the downstairs phone hanging up. "Nina, I am *such* a failure."

"What do you mean?"

"I can't do it," said Marty. "I just can't lie to Mr. Truesdale." She still wasn't sure how she felt about him thinking that she couldn't hear well, either.

"That's not what you said before," Nina said.

"Yeah . . . but—"

"I'm telling you," said Nina, "he's so easy. It was a snap when I did it."

"That's just it," Marty said. "How can I lie to someone that nice?"

"You're forgetting that it's for a good cause," Nina told her. "Gordon and Guardino—Truesdale's pets. Remember?"

"Yeah, but—"

"Tell me something," Nina said. "Is it going to hurt anybody?"

"Well . . ."

"Besides Beverly, I mean?"

"No," Marty said. "Not really."

"See?" said Nina. "And you don't have to go overboard, like learning sign language and everything."

"I know, but . . . don't you think that it's too much like your excuse? You have eye problems. I have ear problems. He might get suspicious."

"Nah!" Nina said. "In fact. In *fact!*" Her voice rose with the wonder of her idea. "This could be a temporary thing —earwax or an infection or something."

"And then what?" Marty said. "When it goes away, I get moved back?"

"By that time," said Nina, "he'll be *so* snowed, *so* crazy about you, that he couldn't bear to send you back."

"Yeah, right!" But Marty loved the idea of it.

"And don't forget," Nina said, "sitting in front is just the first thing. There's all the other stuff we're going to do, too. Getting A's. The book reports with the ribbons. The papier-mâché for extra credit . . ."

Hearing about their plans again perked Marty up a little. Even though they were going to need a *lot* of ribbons for all those book reports he was making them do. They did have some great ideas. Maybe they could do it. Maybe *she* could do it.

"That reminds me," Marty said. "Have you done the homework yet?"

"I'm in the thinking-about-it stage," Nina told her. "I need an inspiration. It has to be super good."

"Yeah," Marty agreed, "our first real assignment."

They had to write a story using the words on their spelling list. And with ones like "glance" and "myth" and "washcloth," it wasn't going to be easy.

"Well, I'd better go," Nina said. "Star Student Nina has to get to work. You, too. Right, Star Student Marty?"

"What?" Marty said. "What? You'll have to speak up, Nina. You know I don't hear very well."

C H A P T E R
Five

So far, Marty had missed about a hundred chances to tell Mr. Truesdale her lie. There had been some good ones, too. Like right now. He was sitting at his desk checking their homework. They were supposed to be reading. But Marty couldn't keep her mind on it. The words seemed to dance on the page.

The backs of Marty's legs stuck to her chair. They made little sucking sounds as she pulled them free. She hoped no one heard. She tucked her skirt under her legs. A *skirt*, two days in a row. She *must* be in love—or completely nuts.

She looked at Mr. Truesdale's beautiful dark head bent over their papers and knew that he'd believe her. It would be so easy, especially since Nina had come up with the idea of telling him it was earwax or an infection. (Marty had decided on earwax.) Saying it was earwax was better than just saying she couldn't hear. And it didn't seem as mean to the people who really couldn't hear very well. She'd been worrying about them.

Marty tried to psych herself up, like she did when she was about to jump into cold water.

Go. Right. Now, she told herself.

It had always worked to get her off the diving board. But it wasn't working now.

If only Nina could do it for her. It would be nothing for Nina.

Just then Nina turned. She gave Marty the high sign and mouthed one word, "Now."

Without thinking, Marty mouthed back, "I can't."

Nina motioned frantically for Marty to come.

Marty shook her head. Beverly had stopped reading and was watching them.

"Come *on!*" Nina mouthed.

Marty shook her head again. There. She'd admitted it. She couldn't do it. She *wouldn't* do it. And this time, Nina wasn't going to talk her into it.

Nina clasped her hands as if she were praying and mouthed, "Ple-e-a-se?"

Marty shook her head, harder this time. "No. No. No," she mouthed.

"Something I can help you with, Ms. Guardino?" It was Mr. Truesdale.

"Um—no . . ." Nina said. "I just—uh—need a—a—tissue."

Mr. Truesdale pointed to a box on the corner of his desk—right in front of Nina.

"Oh . . . yeah." Nina took a tissue. "Thanks." She sniffed noisily into the tissue and wiped at her nose.

Mr. Truesdale went back to checking their homework papers.

Nina threw up her hands and mouthed, "I give up." Then she turned her back and picked up her books again.

Beverly leaned toward Marty. "She's a big liar," she whispered. "She could see perfectly well from here."

Marty pretended she didn't hear. She tried to read again.

Then Beverly closed her book and walked up to Mr. Truesdale's desk. She leaned close to him and talked too quietly for Marty to hear.

Was she telling on Nina?

Mr. Truesdale lifted his head. "Class," he said, "Ms. Bridges has asked if it's all right to read ahead when you've finished the assigned chapter. I'd prefer that you not do so. When you're done, you may read a book of your own or choose one from the class library."

"Thank you, sir." Beverly smiled her most kiss-uppy smile. Then she went back to her seat, took out a fat book, and started reading.

Sir! Beverly had called him "sir." She wasn't just a kiss-up. She was a copycat, too. And asking a question like that was *so* Beverly. At least she hadn't told on Nina. But then, Nina seemed to get away with nearly everything. Maybe it wouldn't be so terrible if just once she got caught. As soon as Marty thought this, though, she felt guilty. How could she wish, even for a second, that Nina would get in trouble?

Marty looked down at her book. It was still open at the first page of the chapter and she had no idea what it was about. A's? How was she going to get even one A if she didn't do the work?

She looked at Nina. Nina was reading, or looked like it anyway. Marty forced her eyes back to the page.

She'd gotten through only two sentences, though, when Mr. Truesdale said, "Finish up the paragraph you're reading and mark your place for next time."

Marty stuck a scrap of paper in her book and slammed it shut.

Mr. Truesdale rose from his desk. "I've looked over your homework papers and I'm pleased," he said. "They're quite good. I wonder if there are any volunteers who'd be willing to read their stories to the class?"

Beverly's hand shot up. But Mr. Truesdale didn't call on her. His blue eyes roved over them.

Marty looked around. She and Nina had promised to raise their hands a lot. But there was no way she was going to do it this time. Frank Fama put up his hand. Then Bernice McCorkle. Then Ernie Norman, over by the windows. Then *Nina. Nina* had her hand up.

"Ms. Guardino." Mr. Truesdale was smiling at Nina. "Would you be the brave one and start us off?"

He rifled through the papers and handed Nina hers.

Marty heard Beverly sigh as she lowered her arm.

Nina got up and stood at the front of the room, facing the class. She didn't even look nervous. She remembered to squint a little, too. "Do you want me to read the title?" she asked Mr. Truesdale.

"If you like."

Nina cleared her throat. "Spelling," she read. Then she laughed.

Everyone else laughed, too, including Mr. Truesdale.

"Ah," he said. "A comedienne. Very good, Ms. Guardino."

Nina smiled at him. She twisted a curl around one finger and let it boing. Then she waited until they were all quiet before she started to read, as if she were giving a speech at a school assembly.

Marty didn't think it was such a hot story, either. It was something about a magic swan. Parts of it didn't even make sense. But she *had* done her homework—which for Nina was like a miracle. And she *had* gone first.

When Nina was through reading, Mr. Truesdale said, "Thank you, Ms. Guardino. And whatever you do, hang on to that title. I think you've got a winner there."

Everyone laughed again. Everyone except Marty, who hadn't thought it was *that* funny to start with. And probably

Beverly. She wouldn't have laughed, either, though Marty didn't check.

"Thank you, sir." Nina smiled at Mr. Truesdale again.

Then she went back to her seat. She only glanced at Marty before sitting down. Score: Nina, a big 1. Marty, nothing.

Next, Frank Fama read something *really* stupid. The name of it was "The Gift of an Odd Washcloth." Marty knew what Frank had done. He'd tried to cram as many spelling words into each sentence as he could. Frank's story was very short. He'd used up three of the words just in the title. Marty had tried that trick before, and it hadn't worked for her, either.

When Beverly got up to read, she said, "I've also used the five challenge words in my story. Was that all right, sir?"

"Of course," he said.

Marty wasn't the only one who groaned. *What* a kiss-up! Mr. Truesdale raised his eyebrows a little, but he didn't say anything about all the groaning.

When Beverly finished reading, Mr. Truesdale said only, "Thank you, Ms. Bridges." Then he looked at the clock. "I'm afraid that'll have to be it for today. I'll leave the rest of your stories here on the desk. Please pick them up on your way out."

Marty flew up the aisle before too many people could see her story. It was right on top of the pile, covered with the usual red pencil marks. She grabbed it up and folded it in half to hide it from Beverly, who stood right by Mr. Truesdale's desk. Beverly was waving her paper in the air, giving everyone the chance to see that it did *not* have any red marks on it.

Marty went back to her desk and pulled out the books she needed for homework. She shoved her story into her notebook without opening it. She'd look at it later. Not now, with nosy Beverly suddenly beside her, arranging her books in a perfect pile. Marty dawdled, waiting to see if Nina would come. Finally, she did.

"You walking?" was all Nina said.

"Yeah." Marty didn't look at Nina but pretended to be searching for something inside her desk. Then, slowly, she gathered up her books and headed to the coatroom for her backpack.

Nina followed. Neither of them spoke a word. They walked out of the building and down the steps.

It wasn't until they were on the sidewalk that Nina said, "So, that's *it*? You're just not going to tell him, *period?*"

Marty pushed back her bangs. "That's what I said."

Nina blew out a long breath. "I can't believe this. After all we planned."

"All *you* planned, you mean."

"You planned it, *too*." Nina's voice was getting louder.

Marty kicked a stone out of her way. "Not the part about changing seats," she said. "That was your idea. I never really wanted to do it."

Nina stopped walking. "Yes, you did," she said. "You're just too chicken."

Marty was. She *was* chicken and it made her feel terrible. But it also hadn't seemed right to lie to Mr. Truesdale. She stopped and turned to face Nina. "I am *not!*"

Nina's hands were on her hips. "You are!" she shouted. "You're a yellow-bellied, chicken-face chicken. That's what you are."

"And you're a big show-off!"

"You're just jealous."

"I am *not*." Now Marty's hands were on *her* hips.

"You are, too," Nina said. "You're jealous because I'm *not* a chicken like you. And Mr. Truesdale likes me. He thinks I'm funny."

"He wouldn't like you if he knew what a liar you are."

Nina's face looked mean. Marty had seen that look before, but never for her.

"Yeah?" Nina yelled. "Well, *you're* a liar, too. You said you'd tell him so you could move your seat. And then you chickened out."

"So?" Marty said. "So . . . what?"

She was too mad to think of anything else to say. She turned and ran toward home as fast as she could. She wanted to be away, far away from Nina's mean look. And she didn't want Nina to see that Marty, the chicken-face chicken, was crying.

Six

By the time Marty got home, she'd managed to stop crying.

But her mother could tell anyway. "What's wrong?" she asked as Marty came through the back door.

Pooh-bah jumped up to greet Marty.

"Nothing." Marty shoved the dog down and tried to get out of the kitchen.

But her mother blocked the way. She put her arms around Marty and drew her in. "What happened?" she asked.

"Nina and I . . . had a . . . fight." As soon as she started talking, the tears began again.

"Oh, honey." Her mother smoothed Marty's hair. "What about?"

"It's so . . . dumb," Marty said. How could she tell her

about the fight without telling her about the lie and *everything*?

"Most fights are dumb," her mother said. "Why don't you talk to me about it?"

"I can't," Marty said. "It's too stupid."

Her mother lifted Marty's bangs from her forehead. "It might make you feel a little better."

Marty pulled away. "No. But thanks, Ma." She wiped her eyes with the back of her hand.

"Well, I hope you two can work it out," her mother said.

Marty knew she meant it, too. Her mother liked Nina. She thought Nina was funny, just like Mr. Truesdale did.

"Yeah, well . . ." Marty hurried upstairs. She wasn't sure that she wanted to work things out with someone who thought she was a yellow-bellied, chicken-face chicken. Even if she *was* one.

"I'm home!" It was Robbie.

Marty closed the door to her room. But she could still hear Pooh's welcoming barks for her brother, and then what sounded like Robbie's voice. He was talking on and on and on, probably telling their mother all about another one of his terrific days at school.

Marty dropped her backpack on the floor. Right about now was when Nina usually called. Sometimes the phone would even be ringing as Marty came in the back door. But not today. And she wasn't going to call Nina, either.

Marty flopped back on the bed. She stared up at the water stain on her ceiling that looked like a big, lumpy cookie.

What was going to happen to all their teacher's-pet plans, now that she and Nina weren't talking? Maybe Marty should just forget about the whole thing. But what if Nina didn't and got to be Mr. Truesdale's pet without her? Marty couldn't let that happen. She'd just have to do all the things they'd planned by herself. But it wouldn't be nearly as much fun without Nina.

Pooh's barking cut into her thoughts. It sounded like he was out in the backyard. Marty got up and went to the window.

"Hush, Pooh!" she yelled through the screen. But he kept racing around the yard in a big circle, yapping.

Robbie and her mother were out there, staring up at the roof. They were probably looking for a good place to put that bat house Robbie had been blabbing about at dinner last night.

Marty got her backpack and brought it to her desk. What could she do to get ahead of Beverly and Nina? To get Mr. Truesdale to think *she* was someone special? She couldn't make anything out of papier-mâché for extra credit yet. Not on the second day of school. And Mr. Truesdale hadn't finished telling them how he wanted them to do their book reports, so she couldn't start one of those. She could buy some fancy ribbons to tie the report covers together the way she'd planned. But somehow that didn't seem like enough.

There was really nothing to do but her homework. She *had* promised to do it every night *and* remember to turn it in. Or had that one been Nina's idea?

Marty began to take her books out of her backpack. There was a knock at her door.

"Marth?" Robbie said in a quiet voice. "Martha?"

"*What* did you call me?"

"Marty," Robbie lied. "Queen Marty. Can I come in?"

"Go away."

"But it's important," Robbie said. *"Please?"*

Marty opened the door a crack. "What?"

He had his bat book again. When Marty saw it, she tried to close the door, but Robbie's foot was in the way.

"No bat stuff," she said. "I'm *not* in the mood."

"But you need to know this," her brother insisted.

Marty went to her desk and straightened her pile of books the way she'd seen Beverly do.

"It's about the house." Robbie put down his bat book and took their father's metal tape measure out of his pocket. "I measured out my bedroom window and the height is just right—fifteen feet straight down with no wires or anything in the way."

"That's great, Rob. I'm sure your bats will be very happy there," Marty said. "Now, get out."

"Well, there's a little problem. . . ." Robbie pulled out the end of the tape measure and let it snap. "Because the bats need a very warm place."

"So?"

Robbie jumped up from the bed and began to pace. "They have to get maximum sunlight, especially in the early morning."

Marty sat down at her desk and pulled up the chair. "Why are you telling me this?"

"Well, my room doesn't face east at all," Robbie said. "It faces west."

"Would you get to the point? I'm trying to do my homework." She'd show Nina who the teacher's pet was going to be. And Beverly, too.

"The best place," Robbie said, "is on the other side."

"What other side?"

"Uh . . . well . . ." Robbie said. "*This* side."

"You mean . . ."

"Yeah, Martha," said Robbie, "right outside your window. But you'll love the bats, once you get used to them."

"Forget it, Robbo." Marty opened her math book and pretended to study the page. "It is *not* going to happen."

"But, Marth . . ."

Marty did not look up. *"Leave."*

"Okay. Okay." Robbie went out and shut the door. "But promise you'll think about it?"

"No!"

Marty buried her face in her hands. Mr. Truesdale hardly knew she was alive. Her best friend hated her. And now her brother wanted to put a bat house right outside her bedroom window—a house for more than a *hundred* bats. Well, she might not be able to do anything about Mr. Truesdale or Nina, but Robbie was *not* going to put that house up outside her window. No way.

Seven

---- ✳ ----

The next morning Marty left home later than usual. She was hoping to keep from meeting Nina on the way. She didn't want to hang around in the school yard for very long, either. If she got it right, she'd be there just in time for the bell.

Marty looked down the block. It was empty. So far, so good. She walked a little faster. When she got to Nina's corner, she couldn't help but look. Just as she did, Nina's front door flew open and Nina ran out. She glanced toward the place where Marty was usually waiting—where she was right now. Nina looked right at Marty. And she knew Marty saw her, too. Marty could tell. But Nina didn't call or wave. And Marty didn't wait. She stared straight ahead and walked very fast, the way kids do when a teacher yells "No running!" in the halls at school.

Marty hated that Nina was behind her, where she could watch her all the way.

By the time Marty got to school, there were tiny rivers of sweat rolling down her sides under her skirt. But she didn't slow down. The school yard was empty. The first bell must have already rung. She ran up the stairs, through the red doors, and down the hall to the classroom. She pulled out her books and the homework she'd worked on so hard. Then she threw her backpack into the coatroom, rushing to get to her seat before Nina came. For once, she was glad to be sitting in the back. Now she'd be the one to do the watching.

The last bell was ringing as Nina ran into the room.

"Just made it, Ms. Guardino," Mr. Truesdale said above the class's racket.

"Better late than never, sir." Nina got out her books and hung her backpack on her chair.

Marty couldn't see, but she bet that Nina was giving Mr. Truesdale one of her best smiles.

Sir, this. Sir, that. Using "sir" had been Marty's idea. And now it seemed that between Beverly and Nina, it might get worn out before Marty had the chance to say it at all.

After taking attendance and the lunch orders, Mr. Truesdale gave them a list of suggested books for their book reports that did *not* include any Nancy Drews or Baby-sitters Clubs.

Marty looked over at Beverly. Beverly was making notes on her list with a perfectly sharpened pencil. She'd probably already read all the books and would have to start on the sixth grade list—for extra credit, of course.

At least Marty knew that Nina wasn't ahead of her in the book-reading department. Nina never read a book unless she absolutely had to. She always said she couldn't see why anyone would bother when all the best ones were made into movies.

Next, Mr. Truesdale taught a lesson on using adverbs. Marty leaned forward, giving him her completely attentive look as he talked. But when he asked them to give examples, she didn't put up her hand. The only adverbs she could think of had to do with him. Ones like "incredibly," as in "incredibly cute," or "unbelievably," as in "unbelievably gorgeous," or "wonderfully," as in "wonderfully nice." Marty noticed that Nina didn't put up her hand, either. Maybe she was having the same trouble that Marty was. Luckily, the work sheet that Mr. Truesdale gave them to do was multiple choice. And it didn't have one adverb on it that reminded Marty of him.

After that was math.

"Based on yesterday's test results, I've assigned you to a math group," Mr. Truesdale said. "Of course, these groupings may change as I get to know your work better."

Mr. Truesdale talked with one foot up on his chair. Today he was wearing a light blue shirt and a blue-and-white-striped tie. Same jacket, same chinos as yesterday, or ones just like them. Even when he was giving them bad news, he looked terrific.

Marty waited to hear her name called. But she had to sit through Mr. Truesdale calling the Math Brain Group, including David DeVoe and, of course, Beverly. Then he called a couple of other groups before he got to hers—the Math Dummies. Nina was in the group, too, which usually helped. But today it didn't. *Nina!* What if they had to sit together?

But, no. Mr. T. (Marty had just decided to call him Mr. T.—but only to herself) came through again. He said he'd call them up only for short lessons or to check their papers. The rest of the time, they could work at their desks.

Mr. T. had said that maybe he'd change their groups later. He'd said that because he didn't know them. But Marty knew. The groups would never change. Oh, maybe the middle ones would shift around a little. But that would be it. That's the way it always was. Some teachers called them Level One and Level Two and Level Three. And other ones called them the Red Birds and the Blue Birds and the Yellow Birds. But they weren't fooling anybody. The kids knew which ones were the smart groups and the stupid groups and the in-between groups—even the kindergartners knew.

Marty felt pretty good doing the math that Mr. T. gave them. There were no word problems, which was a break. They were the worst.

Marty looked at Nina. Even though she was still mad at her, she was dying to tell Nina about her new nickname for

Mr. Truesdale. *Mr. T.* She knew Nina would love it. She'd probably start calling him that, too. They both would. But only with each other. The Nina Marty wanted to tell, though, was the old Nina—the Nina who did *not* call her a chicken-face chicken or give her that mean look. Marty wanted the old Nina back.

"Ms. Gordon's group, please."

It was Mr. T. He was calling Marty's group to the table. He had called their group by *her* name. Maybe he did think she was special. That was something, wasn't it? Even if it was the dummy math group that he'd named for her.

Then Nina turned to Marty with a smirk. She rolled her big liar eyes. And suddenly Marty didn't want to tell her anything—ever again.

Eight

Nina got to the math table first. Marty dawdled at her desk, waiting for the seats around Nina to fill up.

"Ms. Gordon?" Mr. T. was looking at her. "Are you going to join us?"

"Yes, *sir*." There. She'd said it.

Marty hurried to the table and sat in the last empty chair. It scraped on the floor as she scooted in. She glanced at Nina and caught her staring. Marty looked away.

Mr. T. was reviewing long division. He nearly covered the board with numbers. They'd had it last year, but Marty had never really gotten it.

Marty knew she should be paying attention, but the effort of trying not to look at Nina filled up her whole brain.

"Ms. Gordon"—Mr. T.'s voice broke in—"would you care to try one on the board?"

"Uh . . ." Marty felt her face flush as if she had a fever. "No, thank you . . . sir."

"No?" Mr. T. raised his eyebrows in that cute, cute way he had. Then he shifted his gaze to Nina. "Ms. Guardino?"

"Um . . ." Nina looked panicked. "Could you do that last one over again—uh—sir?"

Ha! Nina hadn't been paying attention, either.

But Mr. T. didn't give them a lecture about daydreaming. He just said, "Perhaps we could use a few more examples."

He erased the problems he'd already done and took them through the steps again. This time, Marty *really* listened, but she still didn't get it.

When he was finished, Mr. T. looked at them. "Clearer now?"

The others nodded, even Nina. But Marty didn't have a clue.

Mr. T. must have noticed Marty's blank stare, because when he said, "Anyone who'd like some more help with this can see me at lunch or after school," he looked straight at her.

Did Nina see?

When Mr. T. dismissed them, Marty grabbed her stuff and rushed back to her seat. She decided right then. She'd stay in at lunch. That way, she wouldn't have to find someone to sit with and she'd have Mr. T. all to herself. Maybe she'd even finally learn how to do long division.

Then the lunch bell rang. The rest of the kids hurried out. When Nina left, she wasn't walking with anyone. Who would *she* sit with? Marty wondered.

Mr. T. stood up and started toward the door. Marty had taken only one step in his direction when Beverly ran up. She walked next to Mr. T., looking at him adoringly and talking. Marty had to get to him before he was gone.

"Mr. T.—I mean, Mr. Truesdale," Marty stammered.

But he was listening to Beverly and didn't hear her.

Marty caught up to them just outside the doorway. "Mr. Truesdale." Her voice came out louder than she meant it to.

He stopped. "Yes, Ms. Gordon."

"I—uh—need some help with long division."

He turned to Beverly. "Have a good lunch, Ms. Bridges."

"Oh." Beverly shot a killer look at Marty. "Oh, you, too, Mr. Truesdale." She gave Marty another look over her shoulder as she went down the hall.

"You said . . ." Marty began.

"Sure," said Mr. T. "Want to do it now?"

"Well . . . if it's okay. I mean . . ."

Mr. T. put his hand on her arm. "It's okay. My idea, remember? Just let me grab my lunch from the teachers' room and I'll be right with you."

Then he left. Marty stared at the place on her arm where Mr. T.'s hand had been. He'd touched her. Mr. T. had actually touched her. She had to remind herself to keep breathing.

Nina would die if she knew. She would absolutely *die*. If only Marty could tell her. What good was having something wonderful happen to you if there was no one to tell about it?

"All set?" Mr. T. was back, carrying a brown paper bag.

"Oh . . . yeah . . " Marty hadn't moved from the spot. "I guess I need my—uh—lunch."

Mr. T. nodded.

Marty went to the coatroom and dug her lunch out of her backpack. It was Friday, but they weren't having pizza in the lunchroom, so she'd brought her lunch from home. When she got to the front of the room, Mr. T. was half sitting on the corner of his desk. He was eating what smelled like an Italian sub. There was a can of root beer next to him—regular, not diet. Maybe Nina had been right about the girlfriend.

"I hope you don't mind that I've gone ahead." Mr. T. held up his sandwich.

He talked to her as if she were a real person.

"Uh-uh," Marty said. She couldn't imagine minding anything that he did.

"Shall we take it from the top?" Mr. T. took a sip of his root beer and put it back down on the desk. Then he wrote the first long division problem on the board.

Marty leaned forward in her chair. She wanted him to see how ready to learn she was.

He explained the problem to her, one step at a time. After each part, he stopped and turned to her. "Okay?" he asked.

Marty nodded. She'd never tried so hard to understand anything in her whole life. She thought her brain would break.

After he'd finished the third problem, Mr. T. said, "Now it's your turn."

He put a new one on the board.

Marty gripped the edge of the table.

Mr. T. held out the chalk to her. "Go to it."

She stood and walked to the board on legs that had gone all wobbly. It took her a few tries to figure out how many times 24 went into 58. But she finally got it.

"So far, so good." Mr. T. stood behind her.

Marty didn't dare turn to look. But he was so close. She could feel the warmth of him. She did the next step. Then she waited, holding the chalk in sweaty fingers.

"Go on," Mr. T. said. "You're doing fine."

Fine? She'd *never* been so nervous. Somehow, though, she kept going. And Mr. T. kept saying "Okay." Actually, what he said was "Okay," "Go ahead," "That's right," and "You've got it," in that order. Marty planned to remember every word he said to her—forever.

"There," Mr. T. said when Marty finally got the answer. "That's all there is to it."

Marty turned to him. He was smiling. She smiled back.

Then a voice came from the doorway. "Oh—uh—you're busy." It was *Nina.* "Sorry."

"Your friend, Ms. Gordon, was just finishing up." Mr. T. had a smile for Nina, too.

Friend. He thought they were still friends.

Nina didn't smile though. She said, "I'll come back later." Then she bolted down the hall.

Nina had *seen* them together.

Mr. T. shrugged. He turned to Marty. "Hey," he said, "you haven't touched your lunch."

"Oh . . ." Marty had forgotten about it. It was as if the rest of the world had dropped away, leaving just Mr. T. and her and a chalkboard full of long division.

She felt shy about eating in front of him. She waited until he'd turned to erase the board before she unwrapped her sandwich. She did it as quietly as she could. Then she took a tiny bite and chewed very slowly.

Mr. T. turned to look at her. Marty swallowed hard.

"Think you've got it now?" he asked.

Marty nodded. She had done it once, but she had no idea if she could ever do it again.

Mr. T. put down the eraser and picked up the teacher's edition of the math book. He flipped through the pages. "I want you to do page six for practice tonight," he said. "Just the even-numbered ones. Okay?"

Marty's mouth was full. She nodded again. He could have assigned the whole book and she would have nodded. She tried to chew without moving her mouth too much.

Mr. T. leaned against his desk. "It was brave of you to ask for help, Ms. Gordon," he said. "Most students don't like to admit that they need it."

"M-m-mph." Marty couldn't look at him. She stuffed the rest of her sandwich into its little waxed paper bag.

Brave. He'd said she was brave.

"I guess math doesn't come as easily to you as writing does." Mr. T. drained the last drops of his root beer and set down the can.

"What?" Marty balled up her lunch bag, sandwich and all.

"Your writing," he said. "It's great. I loved your first story." He tossed his sandwich wrapper into the wastebasket.

"You *did?*" Marty remembered jamming the story into her notebook to hide its red marks from Beverly. She'd forgotten all about it.

"Very much," Mr. T. said.

The bell rang for the end of lunch.

Marty stood, with her squished-up sandwich in her hand. "Well—uh—thanks," she managed to say.

Then she fled to the coatroom, her face on fire. She couldn't wait to look at her story.

Nine

On Monday, Marty walked to school alone again. But it wasn't as bad as Friday. For one thing, she didn't run into Nina. And she felt different, too. Bouncier, somehow.

Over the weekend, she must have read what Mr. T. had written on her story a thousand times. And every time she read it, she imagined him saying the words out loud. He'd look at her with those blue, blue eyes of his and say, "Wonderful story, Ms. Gordon. You have a great imagination!"

She'd added the "Ms. Gordon" part. He hadn't actually written it on her paper. She loved it when he called her that, though. It made her sound so grown-up.

A *great* imagination! *She* had one. Mr. T. said so. Remembering that had helped her get through the weekend without Nina. And with Robbie bugging her about his bat house, too. But she hadn't given in, even though Robbie had promised to walk the dog every day forever if only she would. He was wasting his breath. She'd never say yes to a hundred bats right outside her bedroom window.

"*More* than a hundred, if we're lucky," Robbie kept reminding her.

But every time her brother *really* started getting on her nerves, Marty just read those wonderful words of Mr. T.'s.

The teachers she had before Mr. Truesdale were so worried about the kids spelling all the words right and remembering to put in the capitals and the periods. They hadn't even noticed how great Marty's imagination was. And some teachers hadn't had them write made-up stories at all, just ones about What I Did on My Summer Vacation and other boring, real-life things.

When she'd shown her "Agnes, the Nervous Ant" story at the dinner table on Friday night, her father had noticed all the red marks for misspelled words. But after he'd read it, even *he* said that it was pretty good. He liked the stuff Mr. T. had written, too. Her mother had said that making an ant the main character in a story was a very creative idea. Robbie had asked Marty a lot of questions about ants, none of which she'd had an answer for. She'd tried to explain to him that Agnes wasn't a real ant. But that hadn't shut him up. She was kind of sorry she'd ever shown him her story.

✤ ✤ ✤

When she got to school, Marty felt a little funny about seeing Mr. T. at first. But he looked the same—gorgeous.

Of course, no one at school knew a thing. To them, Marty probably still seemed like the same old Marty. But *she* knew she was the girl who'd written a "wonderful story." It was like having a secret identity—one that only she and Mr. T. knew about.

At math time, Mr. T. went over long division again with Marty's group. The lesson at lunch on Friday and the extra problems for practice had helped. Now she sort of got it. But she still hoped he wouldn't call on her. She wasn't ready for that yet.

Nina seemed to be pretending that Marty was invisible. So Marty pretended that Nina was, too.

When math was over, they did social studies and then some science stuff. Half of Marty wished that Mr. T. would assign another story for them to write, and the other half of her wished just as hard that he wouldn't. What if she'd used up her entire great imagination on that one story?

After he'd given them their science homework, Mr. T. said, "Mrs. Luciano had some news for me this morning."

The whole class froze in their seats at the mention of the Dragon Lady's name.

"It seems," Mr. T. went on, "that it's our room's turn to decorate the bulletin board in the hall. Do I have any volunteers?"

Marty's hand shot up for the first time since school had started. This could be her chance to get ahead in the race to be Mr. T.'s pet. But she wasn't the only one. Just about everyone else put his or her other hand up, too. Beverly was waving hers like mad.

"Well, this is certainly an enthusiastic response," Mr. T. said. "But I'm afraid I can use only two or three of you. I guess I'll have to put all your names in a hat."

He was *so* fair, Marty thought. Any other teacher would have just picked his favorites.

"Everyone who is interested, please pass up a scrap of paper with your name on it," Mr. T. told them. "Would one of you let me use your baseball cap?"

David DeVoe went to get his. There was sure to be enough room for all their names in a hat that fit his big, brainy head.

When he had all the names in David's hat, Mr. T. smiled at them. "Gee," he said, "this is kind of exciting." He swished the scraps around and pulled one out. He unfolded the paper and read, "Ms. Bridges."

A big groan went up from the class.

"Jealous," Marty heard Beverly say.

"Good sports, now," Mr. T. said to them. "Let's be good sports." He scrambled their names around again. One fell out onto the floor—a tiny square. "We'll go with this one." He picked it up and unfolded it once, twice, three times. "And it's another lady," he finally said. "Ms. Guardino."

Nina clapped her hands. Then she must have remembered who her partner would be. She turned and gave Beverly a dirty look. Beverly gave her a dirty look back.

"And one more," Mr. T. said. "Let's see if we can get a boy this time." He stirred their names around with his eyes closed. Then he took one out and unfolded it. "Looks like Mr. Fama is the lucky man."

"Wimpy Frankie, working with the little girls," some boy taunted from the other side of the room.

Frank cleared his throat. "Uh—no thank you, Mr. Truesdale," he said.

Mr. T. raised his eyebrows. "Are you going to let one heckler decide for you, Mr. Fama?"

"It's not that." Frank stared at his shoes.

"I'm sure you have a lot to contribute," Mr. Truesdale said.

Frank shrugged. He didn't lift his eyes to look at Mr. T.

"Perhaps next time." Mr. Truesdale didn't sound pleased. "Would you like to choose your replacement, Mr. Fama?"

Frank looked up. He glanced around the room. Then he pointed—to Marty.

Marty stared dumbly back at Frank.

"Well," Frank said, "do you want to or not?"

Everyone was waiting. It felt like a fist was squeezing Marty's heart.

She'd have to work with Beverly. *And* Nina.

But maybe if they were together again, Nina would realize how much she missed her, too. Maybe they'd make up.

Marty shrugged. "Okay."

"Fine," said Mr. Truesdale. "You can begin at lunchtime tomorrow."

C H A P T E R

Ten

Since Frank had picked her yesterday, Marty had gone back and forth and back and forth about what to do.

She'd thought of telling Mr. T. she didn't want to do the bulletin board anymore, that she'd changed her mind, or that her mother wouldn't let her stay after school. Then she'd be out of it. She wouldn't have to keep wondering what it was going to be like working with Nina. And she wouldn't have to deal with kiss-up Beverly, either.

But backing out would leave the whole project to Nina and Beverly. It would give them even more of a chance to impress Mr. T.—a chance Marty would miss if she weren't there.

So she decided to stick with it. But as it got closer to lunchtime, she was less and less sure of her decision.

69

When the bell finally rang, the class raced for their backpacks and headed for the lunchroom. But Marty sat in her chair, arranging and rearranging her books and papers, not looking up.

It got quiet as the room emptied. When Marty lifted her head, the only ones left were her and Beverly and Nina and Mr. T.

Mr. T. took his jacket from the back of his chair and put it on. "Is our bulletin board committee raring to go?" he asked.

"I am . . . sir." Beverly stood and walked to the front of the room.

Marty nodded. She saw Nina nodding, too. Nina got up and stood by Mr. T. But Marty stayed in her seat.

"Ms. Bridges," Mr. T. said, "run next door and see if Mrs. Luciano is still there. She has some letter stencils she said we could borrow."

"Yes, sir." Beverly smiled at Mr. T. and hurried out.

"I have no particular plan in mind." Mr. T. looked first at Nina and then at Marty. "Something about fall or back to school, maybe? You come up with an idea. Just check it with me before you get started."

Marty and Nina nodded some more.

"Well," Mr. T. said, "you know where to find me." He started out the door. Then he paused. "Oh, and Ms. Gordon"—he looked right at Marty—"don't forget to eat your lunch this time."

He left.

"What did he mean by that?" Beverly was back with a big manila envelope.

"Oh . . . nothing," Marty said. She could feel herself blushing. He'd remembered all the way from last week. "It's just—a—private joke."

"A private joke with Mr. Truesdale?" Beverly looked *very* interested.

Nina must be dying to know, too. But she didn't ask. And Marty didn't say anything more. She got up and walked to the table where Nina was already sitting. She pulled out a chair across from her and sat down.

Beverly put Mrs. Luciano's envelope down in front of them. "Well, let's get to work," she said. She sat at the head of the table, as if she were in charge. "I already have some good ideas."

"This is a *committee*, Beverly," Nina told her. "We *all* have to agree."

Marty nodded again. She was beginning to feel like one of those bobble-head dolls who could do nothing *but* nod.

"Well, *you* don't have any ideas, do you?" Beverly looked at Nina.

"That's what we're here for, *Beverly*." Nina twisted a curly strand of hair around one finger. "To think of something."

"I came prepared." Beverly pulled a paper out of the pocket of her skirt and smoothed its creases flat.

"Why don't you ask Marty if *she* has an idea, Beverly?" Nina put her chin in her hands and rested her elbows on the table.

"Well . . ." Beverly turned to Marty. "*Do* you?"

Marty shook her head. She pushed back her chair. "I'm getting my lunch."

The others already had theirs. They must have gotten them before when Marty was busy arranging her stuff.

From the coatroom, Marty heard Beverly's voice, too low to make out.

Then Nina said, "That's the dumbest thing I ever heard of, Beverly. Dumb. Dumb. Dumb."

"What?" Marty came back with her lunch. She addressed her question to the chalkboard, not yet ready to meet Nina's eyes.

"Tell her," Nina said to Beverly. She didn't look at Marty, either.

"Well . . ." Beverly sniffed. "If your friend Nina here seems to think it's *so* dumb . . ."

"*Tell* her."

"All right then." Beverly cleared her throat. Her face got all dreamy. "The picture will be a big globe and the words will say"—Beverly spread her arms in a grand arc as she spoke—"welcome back to Coralwood School, the greatest school on Earth."

"I hate to tell you, *Ms. Bridges,*" Nina said, "but this is *not* the greatest school on Earth."

Beverly's dreamy look disappeared. "How do *you* know it isn't?" she asked. "This is the only school you've ever gone to."

"And it's the only school *you've* ever gone to," Nina said. "How do *you* know it's so great?"

"I just *know*."

"Look at the crummy playground this school's got," Nina said. "Call that the greatest?"

"You *would* think of the playground." Beverly sat up straighter.

"What is *that* supposed to mean?" Nina's voice was rising.

"Nothing"—Beverly fiddled with a corner of Mrs. Luciano's envelope—"but if you cared as much about your schoolwork as you do about the playground, maybe you wouldn't have to *lie* to get the teacher to notice you."

"Are you calling me a liar?"

"You *asked* me what I meant." Beverly put on an innocent look that Marty didn't believe for a minute.

"Well, *you* are a big kiss-up!" Nina yelled.

Suddenly Marty jumped to her feet. She spread her arms wide. "The greatest kiss-up on Earth!" she shouted.

Nina looked at her—surprised. Then she began to laugh. And kept laughing. Marty started, too.

Beverly wasn't laughing, though. "I knew something like this would happen!" she said. She pushed back from the table. "I'm going to tell Mr. Truesdale!"

"Tattletale!" Nina yelled.

Beverly didn't answer. She snatched up the manila envelope as if she were the one in charge of it and stomped off.

"The—greatest—kiss-up—on Earth!" Nina slapped the table. "Did you see Beverly's face?"

"Yeah." Marty had stopped laughing. "But what's Mr. T. going to say?"

"Mr. *T.?* You mean Truesdale?"

"That's what I call him," Marty said. "Not to his face, of course."

"Mr. T." Nina seemed to be trying it out. "Cool."

Marty could tell that Nina loved it, just as she'd known she would.

Marty glanced at the doorway. Empty. And she couldn't hear footsteps. "I just wish he'd come and we could get it over with," she said.

"Well," said Nina, "what can she say? I mean . . . *really?* She isn't going to tell him we called her a kiss-up, is she?" She opened her lunch bag. "We might as well eat."

Marty shrugged. "You never know with Beverly. She doesn't act like a normal person." She unwrapped her tuna on whole wheat.

Nina pulled her sandwich out of its bag, took a bite, and held it up to Marty. "Good ole salami and mayo," she said.

Marty had always thought it was a yucky combination. But it was wonderful to smell its familiar smell again.

Nina smiled at Marty. Even with her mouth full of sandwich, her smile looked like the old Nina's smile.

Marty smiled back. "Good ole salami and mayo," she agreed.

Eleven

———— ✳ ————

Well . . ." Mr. T. walked quickly into the room. "What seems to be the problem here?"

Beverly hurried along beside him with the envelope of stencils held tightly to her chest. "Like I told you, sir," she said to Mr. T. "They're making fun of all my ideas."

"You only had *one*." Nina swept cookie crumbs from the table into her hand and tossed them into her mouth.

Marty wanted to disappear. How much *had* Beverly told him?

"But—" Beverly began.

Mr. T. held up a hand to silence her. *"But,"* he said, "if you can't agree on something, perhaps I should pick a new group for the job."

"Oh, don't do that," Nina said. "We've got so many good ideas—sir."

"Then you may submit them to me anonymously and I'll do the choosing," Mr. T. said. "That's no names. And I want them all at the same time."

"Yes, Mr. Truesdale." Beverly had lost the triumphant look she'd had when she'd first come in.

"Sounds okay to me," Nina said.

Marty nodded.

"Good luck," said Mr. T., and he left.

That was it. Marty couldn't believe it. He hadn't acted mad. Not *really*—a little annoyed, maybe. But he *had* been eating lunch. Maybe Beverly hadn't told him what Marty said. Or maybe she had, and Mr. T. thought Beverly was a kiss-up, too.

Marty looked over at Nina. Nina gave her the thumbs-up sign. She hid it with her other hand so that Beverly couldn't see.

Nina leaned forward. "See, Miss Tattletale, he didn't even care."

Beverly shrugged. She pulled out Mrs. Luciano's stencils and fanned them out on the table like a hand of cards.

"You think you're so smart," Nina said. "But so far, you've only come up with one weird idea. What about all those other ones you said you had?"

Beverly collected the stencils into a pile and straightened them. Then she put them back into the envelope, taking her time. "Oh, I have a *lot* of other ideas." She tucked the

76

flap into the envelope. "But I'm going to give *mine* to Mr. Truesdale. He can choose the one he likes."

"And you think he'll pick *yours*, right?" Nina said.

"Well, he *does* want the best one." Beverly got up and put the envelope on Mr. T.'s desk.

Nina stood. "Like I told Truesdale, we've got some good ideas, too." She looked at Marty. "Right, Marty?"

Marty nodded. Mr. T. might think she had a great imagination. But right now, she didn't have a thought in her head.

The bell rang.

Beverly picked up the lunch bag that she'd never opened. "I'll collect all the ideas in the morning and give them to Mr. Truesdale," she said.

"*I'll* collect them," said Nina.

"Suit yourself." Beverly must be remembering Nina's temper. "Just make sure he gets *all* of them."

The racket in the hall was rising. The other kids were coming back from the playground.

Marty balled up what was left of her lunch and threw it into the wastebasket. Nina blew up her empty bag and popped it with a bang. She and Marty both giggled. Beverly shook her head and rolled her eyes. Then she turned and walked back to her seat without saying another word.

The rest of the afternoon seemed to go on and on. Even though Mr. T. was as adorable as ever, it was hard for Marty to pay attention. She kept thinking about Nina. Was the fight with her *really* over? It seemed like it was. But neither of them had said they were sorry yet. Nina had started the fight. *She* should say it first. Marty would say it second.

Finally, it was three o'clock.

"Don't forget to bring in all your *brilliant* ideas tomorrow, Ms. Gordon," Beverly said as she got up to leave.

Marty didn't answer her. She was wondering what to do. Should she wait for Nina? Should she go up to her and say something?

Math book, notebook, science folder. Marty piled up the things she needed for homework.

Suddenly Nina was standing next to her. "You walking?" she asked.

Marty looked at Nina. Nina was smiling.

"Yeah," Marty said. "Are you?"

"Yeah."

Marty put her books in her backpack. Then she and Nina walked out together.

Twelve

—— ✳ ——

Nina started talking as soon as they got outside, and she kept talking for three blocks straight. She talked about Mr. T.'s tie. How it was blue-and-yellow-striped. No big deal. But how it looked so wonderful on him. She talked about Beverly Bridges—what a complete creep she was. And how she was never going to be anything but a complete creep—*ever*. And about Frank Fama. How he was pretty nerdy but also sort of nice sometimes—like that day he'd let them try on his glasses in the lunchroom and when he'd picked Marty for the committee.

When Nina finally paused to take a breath, Marty stopped walking. "Nina," she said, "is the fight over?"

"Well, yeah." Nina stopped, too. "For *me*. Is it for you?"

"Well"—Marty adjusted the shoulder strap on her backpack—"I want it to be. But you—uh—you never said you were sorry."

"Neither did you." Nina pulled off her headband and her curls boinged out in all directions.

"*You* started it, though," Marty said.

"Not really." Nina turned her headband around in her hands. "First, *you* broke your promise about getting Truesdale to change your seat."

Marty watched the toe of her sneaker as it traced an invisible circle on the sidewalk. "Nina," she said, "you *know* I can't do stuff like that."

"I know," Nina said. "You *are* a terrible liar."

Marty kept her eyes on her sneaker. "I felt awful when you called me all those names."

"Only one," said Nina. "Yellow-bellied, chicken-face chicken is all *one* name. It just has a lot of parts to it."

"It was bad enough not having the guts to talk to Mr. T. . . ." Marty was afraid she might start to cry. "And then . . ."

"Mart, stop." Nina put her hand on Marty's arm. "I *am*, okay? I just can't say it."

"What if I do it with you?" Marty asked. "We'll say it together on the count of three."

"Well . . ." Nina pushed her headband back down into her curls, where it seemed to disappear.

"C'mon, Nina," Marty said. "You don't want to be a yellow-bellied, chicken-face chicken, do you?"

Nina sighed. "Oh . . . all right."

"Ready?"

Nina nodded.

"One, two, three."

"Sorry!" they both said. Then they giggled.

"Okay." Nina started walking again. "The fight's over."

"Completely over." Marty's steps matched Nina's.

They were almost to Nina's street.

"So . . ." Nina said, "want to come to my house?"

"I have to wait for Robbie's bus and stay with him until my mother comes home from the city," Marty said. "Want to come to *mine*?"

"Sure."

They kept walking.

"Do you have any ideas for the bulletin board?" Marty asked. "You told Beverly you did."

"Nah," said Nina. "But I couldn't let *her* know that. Do you have one?"

Marty shook her head.

They turned down the Gordons' driveway. Pooh-bah was in the yard. He threw himself against the chain-link fence, barking happily at their arrival.

"Maybe we should ask Robbie for an idea," Nina said. "He's such a little genius."

"Such an *annoying* little genius." Marty fumbled in her pocket for her key. When she got the back door open, Pooh raced past them into the kitchen. Marty dumped her backpack and headed for the refrigerator.

"Don't worry," Nina said. "We'll come up with something."

Marty slammed the refrigerator door. There was nothing good to eat. "Yeah . . . well . . ."

"Here." Nina took an apple from the basket on the table and tossed it to Marty. "You're not giving up to that creep Beverly, are you?" she asked.

Marty twisted the stem of her apple. She thought of Tattletale Beverly and her perfect sneakers and her perfect pencil and her perfect everything. "No way," she said.

"No way," Nina agreed. "We'll come up with something terrific!"

"Then who'll be Mr. T.'s pets?" Marty asked. "His very favorites in the whole class?"

"*Us!*" Nina raised her hand in the air.

Marty slapped it—a high five. "Yes, *us!*" she yelled.

Great. Now all they had to do was think of something.

Thirteen

———— ✳ ————

Marty and Nina tried all afternoon. But they just couldn't come up with one decent idea for the bulletin board.

"Maybe we're working too hard," Nina said. "Maybe if we relax and forget about it, something will come to us. *Bing!* Like magic."

So they lay down on the living room floor and closed their eyes. But that only sent them into a giggling fit.

Marty was so desperate that, after Nina left, she even asked Robbie. But he was no help.

"It would be a great chance to teach people about bats," Robbie said.

"I *told* you," said Marty, "it's supposed to be something about fall or back to school."

"Okay," Robbie said. "How about 'coming back to school to learn about bats'?"

"You're impossible!" Marty started up the stairs to her room.

Robbie followed her. "Ants?" he said. "What about ants, Marth? You like ants."

Marty didn't answer. She went in her room and shut the door. *ANTS?* It *had* been a mistake to let Robbie read her Agnes story. Marty sat down at her desk. She tapped her pen against her notebook, trying to rev up her great imagination. But all she could think of was Nina. It was great to have her back—to be best friends again. Maybe she'd call Nina—just to see if she'd thought of anything yet. Marty pushed her chair back from the desk. Then she scooted it in again. If she called Nina, they'd never get off the phone. And she had work to do. She'd better start acting like a teacher's pet if she wanted to be one.

But . . . what if she promised to stay on the phone for only a couple of minutes? *One* minute. Absolutely no longer than one minute. Marty got up from her chair and started for the door.

Pooh went into a barking fit.

"I'm home!" Marty's mother called.

Marty opened her door and almost knocked Robbie over.

"Come down here," Mrs. Gordon shouted, "the two of you! Dinner has to be on the table in five minutes."

"What's the big rush?" Marty ran down the stairs with Robbie right behind her.

Pooh-bah, still barking like a maniac, raced ahead to the kitchen.

"Your father has a meeting tonight." Marty's mother took down a stack of plates. "Here, Robbie, set the table, and I don't care whose turn it is."

Robbie sighed. The cycle would be off again. It was supposed to be Marty's night to set the table.

Marty lifted the lid on a flat white box. "Yum, pizza!"

"Put that lid down. It keeps the heat in." Marty's mother bustled around the kitchen with her purse still on her shoulder. "Peel some carrots, will you, Marty?" she said. "There isn't time to make a salad."

"Hello, everybody!" Marty's father came through the back door. "M-m-m-m. Smells like pizza."

Pooh went completely nuts. He seemed to save his most enthusiastic barks for Mr. Gordon.

Marty stood at the sink, peeling carrots. Long orange ribbons of carrot peel flew into the basin. "Hi, Dad," she said.

Her father kissed Marty's cheek. "How's my girl?" He looked around. "Anyone walk Pooh lately?"

Pooh yipped at the mention of his name.

Marty and Robbie looked at each other.

"After dinner," their mother said. She plunked the bowl of carrot sticks that Marty had peeled on the table. "Right now, it's time to eat. Everybody *sit*."

They all did, including Pooh.

"So, how was everyone's day?" Mrs. Gordon asked as she handed out slices of pizza.

85

"Fine. Fine." Marty's father took a slice.

"Nina and I made up," said Marty.

"Honey, that's great." Her mother bit into her pizza.

Marty's father dabbed his mouth with a napkin. "A social life is all well and good," he said. "But remember, Marty, it won't get you into college."

"Dad," Marty said, "I'm only in fifth grade."

"Never too early." Mr. Gordon took another slice of pizza from the box. He was already on his second piece and Marty hadn't even taken a bite of her first. He had to be the world's fastest eater.

"Don't waste your breath, Dad." Robbie waved a carrot stick in the air. "She never pays attention. I just gave her two terrific ideas for her bulletin board at school, but did she listen? No."

"What were your ideas, son?" their father asked.

Marty kicked Robbie under the table. "What else?" she said. "Bats."

"*Or* ants," Robbie said. "And stop kicking me, Martha."

Suddenly Mr. Gordon jumped up. "Look at the time! I'll be late if I don't hurry." He picked up his plate and glass.

"Leave them, Dad," Robbie said. "It's Martha's turn to clear."

"It is *not*." Marty tried to kick Robbie again. But she missed.

Pooh sprang up when Mr. Gordon did and was already whining and making little leaps at the back door.

"Listen to your brother once in a while, Marty." Her father put his dinner dishes in the sink. Then he pushed Pooh aside and opened the back door. "And will someone walk this animal? I've got to go."

Listen to *Robbie?* Her father *had* to be kidding. If she did that, she'd have a hundred bats living under her window, and who knew what else?

"I'll walk Pooh if you'll do the dishes," Marty told Robbie.

"No way." Robbie pushed his chair back from the table. "*I'll* walk him."

Marty couldn't believe that someone who was supposed to be as smart as Robbie always fell for that same trick. She hated walking the dog.

Pooh wagged his whole body when he saw Robbie with his leash.

"Be firm, Robbie," their mother said. "Show him who's boss."

"I will," Robbie promised and he probably meant it. But the dog was already dragging him out the door.

Mrs. Gordon took a sip of her tea. "So, what's this about a school bulletin board?"

"Oh." Marty started to clear the table. "We're supposed to think of an idea and bring it in tomorrow. The teacher's going to pick the best one." She rinsed the plates and put them in the dishwasher. "Actually, Nina and I are going in together."

"Well," her mother said, "between the two of you, I'm sure you'll come up with a good one."

Marty finished loading the dishwasher and closed the door. "Maybe."

She left the kitchen and went upstairs. She sat down at her desk again. But all she had was the urge to call Nina.

There was a quiet knock at her door. "Marth?" Robbie was back from walking the dog. "If you'll just take a look at this one picture, it might change your mind." He slid a booklet with a bat on the cover under the door.

"How many times do I have to tell you?" Marty shot the booklet back to Robbie's side. "I am *not* interested."

"An ant one, then?" Robbie asked. "I found a really neat ant one today."

"Leave, *now!*"

"You and Nina. Nina and you," Robbie shouted. "That's all you ever think about." He slammed the door to his room.

Marty flung her door open. "Well, it's a lot better than *bats*, or—or *ants!*" She slammed her door, too. Then, she lay down on her bed, slumped against the headboard.

Robbie was *such* a little jerk. But he *was* right about one thing. She *couldn't* stop thinking about Nina and how great it was to be best friends with her again.

Suddenly Marty sat straight up. That was it. *Friends.* That could be her idea for the bulletin board. She wasn't the only one who cared about her friends. Most kids did. Well, not Beverly . . . she didn't *have* any friends. But for all the other kids, being with their friends was one of the best things about school. It was almost worth coming back from summer vacation for.

On the bulletin board, she could put up lots of pictures of the kids at Coralwood. Everyone in their class could be up there, maybe everyone in the school. The teachers could even have their pictures on the board, if they wanted to. The background would be blue, just like the sky, with big letters in all colors, curving over the pictures like a rainbow. She'd use Mrs. Luciano's stencils to make the letters look perfect. And the words would say . . . Coralwood Friends, Together Again.

Marty could just see all the kids crowding around, trying to find their pictures and all their friends' pictures, too.

She jumped up and headed for the phone. Wait till Nina heard about her idea.

There was no way Beverly would ever come up with one to beat it . . . was there?

Fourteen

———— ☆ ————

They'd rushed through their lunches, and now the committee—Marty, Nina, and Beverly—sat around the table. They watched the door and waited. Mr. Truesdale should be back with his decision about the bulletin board any minute.

Finally he came in. "Sorry to take so long," he said. He smiled one of his incredible smiles. "This was a tough choice. All the ideas were good ones."

All? How many *had* there been in that fat envelope that Beverly had given Nina that morning?

Mr. T. reached inside his jacket pocket and took out a paper. He unfolded it slowly.

Please. Please. Please. Marty closed her eyes and sent up a silent prayer.

"I chose this one," Mr. T. said.

Marty opened her eyes. Her sketch was in his hand.

Nina let out a little whoop and clapped Marty on the back. "Way to go, Mart."

Marty looked down at the table, trying not to smile and smiling anyway. He'd picked *her* idea.

"Ah, Ms. Gordon," Mr. T. said. "Congratulations. I think this project will be a lot of fun for the students."

"Fun?" Beverly practically snorted. "I thought it was supposed to be *educational*. . . ." Then her voice got much nicer. "Sir."

"Educational?" Mr. T. said. "Well, I don't know about that. But it is welcoming. And as one of the newcomers around here, I like that very much."

He said he liked it. He liked it *very* much.

"First, we have to collect all the pictures," Nina said.

"Why don't you write up a notice about that, Ms. Gordon?" asked Mr. T.

Marty lifted her eyes to find his blue, blue ones looking right at her.

"I'll have it copied and we'll get it out this afternoon." He straightened his tie—his perfect tie.

Marty nodded. She could do it. Right now, she could do almost anything.

"I'll leave you to your work, then." Mr. T. smiled at them before he left.

"I'll start tracing the letters." Nina got up.

91

Beverly leapt from her chair. "*I'll* get the stencils," she said. "I know just where they are."

Marty and Nina exchanged looks.

"Then *I'll* get the colored paper." Nina went to the art supply cabinet.

Beverly was acting as if she were in charge again. Marty didn't really care, though. Beverly could be as bossy as she wanted. But it was going to be Marty's idea up there on the bulletin board. The one Mr. T. thought was the best.

"We should have red paper in the background so that the pictures will stand out," Beverly said in her know-it-all voice.

"Blue," said Nina. "Marty said sky blue." She turned to Marty. "Right, Mart?"

"Right." Marty wasn't used to people asking her what to do, especially Nina.

"Then *I'll* go get some of that paper off the big roll in the teachers' room." Beverly looked at Marty. "Blue, if you insist. But it's not going to look right." She left in a huff.

"Ha!" Nina said as soon as Beverly was out the door. "Did you see her face? She can't believe Mr. T. didn't pick one of *her* dumb ideas."

"I know." Marty could hardly believe it herself.

Nina flipped through a stack of construction paper. "So, what color do you want the first word to be?"

"Start with a purple word," Marty said. "Then blue, then green, and keep going till you use up all the colors in the rainbow."

"But there are only four words." Nina began to pull purple sheets from the pile.

"Well, we've only got construction paper in six of the rainbow colors," Marty said. "They never have indigo. So let's count the letters and divide them by six. Then we'll have an even number of letters for each color."

"You're a brain, you know it?" said Nina. "Counting up and dividing? You better watch it or Truesdale will move you out of the Math Dummies."

Marty shook her head. "Never." Then she wrote *Coralwood Friends, Together Again* on a piece of paper and counted the letters. "Twenty-nine," she told Nina. "Rats! It won't come out even if we divided them by six."

Nina leaned over the paper, her head almost touching Marty's. "It will if we count the comma," she said. "Then we can divide six into thirty."

"You're a genius!" Marty said. "Maybe *you'll* be the one to get moved out of the Math Dummies."

They both laughed.

"What's so funny?" Beverly was back, dragging a big roll of blue paper.

"Nothing," Nina and Marty both said at the same time. Then they laughed again.

Beverly glared at them. She held up the roll of paper. "It looks as bad as I thought, but it's what you wanted." She tossed the paper onto the table.

"Why don't you put it up on the board?" Nina said. "Marty's got to do that notice. You know, the one that Mr.

Truesdale asked *her* to write, *special?* And *I'm* doing the letters."

"Fine." Beverly sounded far from fine. She picked up the roll of paper and Mr. T.'s stapler and went out into the hall.

When Marty finished writing the notice, she helped Nina trace letters. Then came the hard part—cutting them out. She wanted them to look perfect and it wasn't going to be easy with the crummy school scissors they had.

Nina picked up her scissors. "I had a great idea for the bulletin board that I never handed in," she said.

"I thought you couldn't think of anything." Marty concentrated on the red *a* she was cutting out.

"Wait'll you see this." Nina lay down her scissors and dug in her pocket. She pulled out a paper and handed it to Marty.

Marty unfolded it. "Oh, *Nina!*"

It was a drawing of a man in a bathing suit. He had bulging muscles and a big smile. Over the drawing were the words "Mr. Truesdale, the Greatest Hunk on Earth."

"Think I should have turned it in?" Nina asked.

"You couldn't," Marty said. "It has your name on it."

They both collapsed in laughter.

"And—and—you know who gave me the idea?" Nina could hardly get out the words.

"Who?"

"*Beverly*," Nina said. "Beverly with her corny bulletin board idea. Remember?" Nina jumped from her chair and swept her arms wide. " 'Welcome back to Coralwood

School—the greatest school on Earth'! I actually got the idea from *Beverly*."

"Let me *see* that." Beverly snatched Nina's drawing out of Marty's hand.

She must have snuck up from behind.

"Hey, give that back." Nina lunged across the table.

"I will *not!*" Beverly ran for the door.

Nina raced around the table, dodging chairs. The bell rang. At the doorway, Beverly ran straight into Mr. T. Nina stopped short, just behind her.

"Whoa!" Mr. T. said. "What have we here, a game of tag?"

"Uh—no—sir," Beverly said. "I was—uh—just—uh . . ."

"Coming to tell you how we were doing," Nina finished in an incredibly normal-sounding voice.

"It looks as if most of the committee were coming." Mr. T. nodded at Nina. "So, how *are* you doing?" He walked toward the front of the room.

"Fine," Marty lied.

"That's good to hear." Mr. T. walked over to the table. He looked approvingly at the letter cutouts. "I hope you've finished with the stencils," he said. "Mrs. Luciano needs them back this afternoon."

"Oh . . . yes." Marty gathered the stencils and stuffed them into the envelope. "We're all done. They're right . . . here." She held the envelope out to Mr. T.

Marty glanced at Beverly. Beverly's eyes were on Nina. Beverly was making a big show of slowly folding Nina's drawing over and over until it was a tiny square. Nina looked ready to pounce.

Beverly tucked the folded square into her fist and held it there, out of sight, the way kids do when they're playing guess which hand. What if Beverly showed Nina's drawing to Mr. T.?

Marty could hear the other kids coming up the stairs from recess.

"Ms. Bridges," Mr. T. said, "would you return these to Mrs. Luciano?" He handed her the stencils.

"Of course, sir." Beverly took the envelope with her free hand. She started out the doorway. But then she turned. She smiled her meanest smile as she dropped the paper with Nina's great idea into Mrs. Luciano's envelope.

Fifteen

———— ✳ ————

When Mr. T. turned his back, Nina grabbed for Beverly. But she missed, and Beverly was out the door with Mrs. Luciano's envelope *and* Nina's great idea.

Then the bell rang for the end of lunch, and Mr. T. called them to their seats.

When Beverly came back from Mrs. Luciano's, she slid into her chair without looking at Marty.

"You're a *jerk*, Beverly," Marty whispered, "a *really* big jerk."

Beverly acted as if she didn't hear.

An hour and a half passed, and nothing happened. Nothing except that Nina kept turning around. When she wasn't making frantic faces at Marty, she was giving her mean look to Beverly. But Beverly ignored her.

Mr. T. assigned another spelling-word story for them to write. It was due the next day. Marty looked at the list of words—"prince," "cloak," "frozen," "oatmeal," and a bunch of others. Frank Fama was bound to come up with another weird one with those. None of the words on the list gave Marty an idea for a story.

Mr. T. talked about their first book reports. He reminded them that they had to bring in a nonfiction book for approval tomorrow. *Tomorrow.* Marty hadn't picked a book yet. She couldn't even remember where her list was.

Nina turned around again. She pointed to the clock on the wall. Then she folded her hands in prayer. "Please," she mouthed, "ple-e-ease."

The dismissal bell would ring in fifteen minutes. If they could just make it till then, they'd be safe—at least for today.

Then Mrs. Luciano appeared in the doorway. "Mr. Truesdale," she said, "could I have a word with you?"

"Certainly, Mrs. Luciano," he said. "Come right in."

Mrs. Luciano beckoned with one finger. *"Privately."*

"Oh, of course." Mr. Truesdale started out. Then he turned to face them. "Excuse me for a moment, class," he said.

The whole room started to buzz as soon as Mr. T. closed the door. As far as Marty could tell, only she and Nina and Beverly knew about the drawing. But everyone else could see that Mrs. Luciano looked *serious*, and you could expect the worst when she looked like that. Only Beverly seemed unconcerned. She took out one of her books and began to read. Or pretended to, anyway.

Nina looked like she was about to have a nervous breakdown, and Marty *felt* like she might have one right along with her. How would they ever face Mr. T. if he saw Nina's drawing?

"What does Luciano want?" Frank Fama asked Marty.

Marty just shrugged.

After what seemed like a very long time, the door opened and Mr. T. strode in. He tucked a folded paper into the inside pocket of his jacket as he walked. "Let's finish up here, shall we?" he said. He didn't look at Nina or at anyone in particular.

If only Marty had X-ray eyes and could see what was in Mr. T.'s pocket.

"Ms. Gordon." Mr. T. held out a stack of papers. "You'll need to hurry if these are going home today. Take someone with you. It'll go faster."

The notices about bringing in pictures for the bulletin board! After Marty had given him the letter she'd written at lunchtime, she'd forgotten all about them. "Nina?" she said.

Nina leaped from her seat and sprinted for the door. "Oh, Mart!" she said as soon as they were in the hall. "He's got it. I bet Luciano gave it to him."

"I *know*." Marty thrust some of the notices at Nina. "But

take these and hurry or we won't make it before the bell."

"*You* take Luciano's," Nina said.

"Of course," Marty said. "You do the little kids' hall."

Nina disappeared through the swinging doors.

Mrs. Luciano was yelling at her class about something when Marty went in. She saw Marty and stopped long enough to raise one dark, penciled eyebrow.

"Please give these out today," Marty said. She threw the notices on Mrs. Luciano's desk and fled.

The dismissal bell rang just as Marty delivered her last batch. When she got back to her classroom, Nina was already in the coatroom, cramming her books into her backpack.

"C'mon," Nina said. *"Hurry!"*

Marty went to her desk to get her stuff. She shoved her books into her backpack and zipped it up.

Nina was at Marty's elbow. "Let's get out of here," she whispered. She hopped around in a little hurry-up dance.

Marty slung her backpack on her shoulder. They started down the hall, walking fast. They were almost to the swinging doors when Mr. T's. voice stopped them.

"Oh, Ms. Guardino," he called, "could I please have a word with you before you go?"

CHAPTER# Sixteen

arty stood in the hall. It seemed to be taking Nina so long. Marty shifted from one foot to the other. She was dying to run. She knew she should want to try to rescue her friend. But what she really wanted to do was run away— as fast and as far as she could. Run away and never come back. Nina was right. Sometimes she *was* a yellow-bellied, chicken-face chicken.

She strained to hear the voices coming from their classroom. But she couldn't make out the words or even tell who was talking.

Then she heard Nina say, "See you tomorrow, sir!"

Nina shrugged on her backpack as she came down the hall toward Marty. "Let's get out of here," she whispered. "I'll tell you outside."

They walked very fast.

The big red doors had not even shut behind them when Nina said, "He's the best. The absolute *best*."

"What do you mean?" Marty asked. "Didn't Luciano show him your picture?"

"Uh-huh. He gave it back." Nina patted her pocket. "I have it right here."

"*So?*"

"So," said Nina, "he said I must *really* be a comedienne if I thought he looked like that in a bathing suit."

"That's *all?*" Marty said. "That's *all* he said?"

"No," said Nina. "He said I should be more careful about who gets to see my jokes. He said everyone doesn't have my sense of humor."

"But weren't you embarrassed?"

Nina shook her head. Then she said, "Well . . . maybe a little."

"I would have wanted to die," Marty said.

"He made it so easy, though," said Nina. "He acted like it was no big thing."

"That's great." Marty sighed. He was *so* wonderful.

"Yeah," Nina said. "Now we can stop worrying about that and concentrate on getting back at that creep Bridges. I can't believe even *she* did something so low."

"What's the worst thing we could do to her?" Marty asked. "She deserves the *worst*."

"We're going to beat her at the only thing she cares about," Nina said, "being Truesdale's pet."

"But we're *already* trying to do that," said Marty. "And we'll never be able to stop her from getting all those A's."

"No," Nina agreed. "But I've been thinking. We could make ourselves look more mature. More *glamorous*. He's bound to notice that. And Beverly's such a Little Miss Prim. She doesn't have a clue about being glamorous."

"What do you mean?" Marty asked. She didn't have a clue, either.

Nina pushed back her headband. "We'll start with makeup," she said. "Have you got any?"

"Not exactly," said Marty.

"Don't worry," Nina said. "My cousin taught me these great tricks to do when you run out of makeup."

"We haven't run out, Nina," Marty said. "We never had any to begin with."

Nina kept walking. "Whatever . . ." She pinched her cheeks. "See?" She turned to Marty. "If you do this real hard, it makes your cheeks pink. Just like wearing blusher."

Marty inspected Nina's cheeks. "Yeah," she said. "It does . . . sort of." Marty pinched her own cheeks. "But it kind of hurts."

Nina pinched her cheeks again. "You get used to it," she said. "Like wearing a girdle or high heels."

Marty hadn't planned on getting used to high heels for a long time, and she'd die before she'd ever wear a girdle. "What other tricks did your cousin teach you?" she asked.

Nina's cousin was in *seventh* grade. She knew a lot of things.

103

"Well," said Nina. "There's the M&M trick."

"I know that one," said Marty. "You lick the red ones and rub them on your lips to make it seem like you're wearing lipstick."

"It looks real, too," Nina said. "You just have to remember not to lick it off."

"It doesn't last that long, though," said Marty. "We've tried it before. Remember?"

"So we buy a *lot* of M&M's." Nina stopped walking. "Honestly, Marty, do you want to beat out Beverly or not?"

"After what she did?" Marty said. "You'd better believe it."

"We'll get the M&M's on the way to school in the morning." Nina started walking again. "And we'll keep up the other things, too. Doing all the homework and raising our hands and stuff."

"Yeah . . ." Marty said, "but . . ." It seemed like such a *lot*.

"We can do it," said Nina. "For tonight, we've got one measly, little spelling word story."

"Have you seen the words?" Marty asked. "They're terrible. And I don't have something picked out for the book report yet, either. I can't even find my list."

Nina shrugged. "You don't need the list," she said. "That's just for fiction. This report's supposed to be nonfiction. Don't you remember? Mr. T. said we could pick any book we wanted. He just has to approve it."

Actually, Marty didn't remember.

"I'm doing Helen Keller," Nina said. "My cousin—the same one who knows the makeup tricks—gave me the book. She said teachers are crazy about Helen Keller."

"How come?"

"Oh, Helen Keller was so smart and nice and everything," Nina said. "That's what my cousin said, anyway. I haven't read the book yet. And Helen Keller was blind and deaf, too. My cousin says you can't lose with her."

Marty nodded. She wished she had an older cousin to give her advice about things.

They got to Nina's corner and had to say good-bye. For once, Nina's mother had insisted that she come right home from school. They couldn't even stand on the corner talking as they usually did.

"Don't forget your picture for the bulletin board!" Nina shouted as she ran down her street. "And your M&M money!"

Her picture for the bulletin board. Marty had forgotten about it. Would the other kids remember to bring their pictures in? Suddenly she imagined something awful—a nearly empty bulletin board. One with faded blue paper and pictures of only her and Nina and a few kindergartners on it. Mr. T. would be sorry he'd ever picked her idea.

"Beep! Beep!" Beverly zoomed by on her bike. She lifted one hand in a wave, but she didn't turn and Marty didn't wave back. Beverly had a pile of books in her bike basket

—at least three. She'd have *her* book in on time. And it was bound to be a good one—maybe even better than one on Helen Keller.

Marty started to run. If she got home fast enough, she could get her mother to take her to the library. It closed at five on Wednesdays. But there was still time. And her mother could help her pick out a book, too.

She ran up the walk to her house. Pooh was barking and pawing at the screen door.

"Ma! Ma!" Marty shouted over the dog's racket. "Can you take me to the library?"

Pooh jumped at her and licked her hands when she tried to push him away.

"Ma's not here!" Robbie yelled from upstairs.

Oh, *great.* Marty was still trying to get past the dog. "When's she coming back?"

"Not late," Robbie said. "She said at least by five."

Marty dropped her backpack and sank into a kitchen chair. Now she wouldn't have her book on time. Nina would have Helen Keller and Beverly would have some other perfect book. And she'd have nothing. All the "lipstick" in the world wouldn't make up for that.

Seventeen

———— ✳ ————

They tried the M&M trick the next morning on the way to school. And it worked. Nina looked like she was wearing real lipstick. She said that Marty did, too.

With the M&M lipstick on, Marty felt more sophisticated. Older. Even if it wasn't real, it almost made up for the way she felt about the book she had for her report.

"So what did you end up getting?" Nina asked.

"Oh, it's a book about some kind of scientist."

"What *kind* of scientist?"

Marty fought an almost overpowering urge to lick her lips. "Oh, he's a guy who knows a lot about . . . bats." She said the last word very quietly.

"Robbie must be happy," Nina said.

"I had no choice," Marty told her. "My mother didn't get

home in time to take me to the library. Robbie was my only hope."

"But you hate bats," Nina said.

"I know." She hoped Mr. T. didn't ask her any questions about her subject.

"I think I'll stick with Helen Keller," Nina said. "What did you bring for the bulletin board?"

"My dorky fourth grade picture."

"Me, too," said Nina. "My mother tried to get me to bring one of me at the beach. But no way was I doing that." She pulled a bunch of leaves from someone's privet hedge as they walked by. "You get your story done?"

"Yeah . . ." Marty tucked her bangs behind one ear, and miraculously, they stayed there. "I don't think it's as good as the ant one, though."

"The guy in mine is a prince who has a magic cloak made of frozen oatmeal." Nina shredded leaves as she talked.

Marty held her head very straight to keep her bangs from falling forward. She practiced not licking her lips. "Doesn't sound too comfortable," she said.

"Yeah, but it's four spelling words in one sentence," Nina pointed out. "You've got to admit *that* part's good."

"Oh, it is." Marty turned to Nina. But she did it too fast and her bangs fell over her eyes.

They were almost to school. Soon she'd know if the other kids liked her bulletin board idea enough to bring their pictures in. She'd never done anything that the whole school knew about before.

The bell was ringing as they came into the school yard. Everyone was heading for the door. She and Nina were the last ones. When they got to their classroom, Marty hesitated. She'd feel like such a jerk if the other kids hadn't brought in their pictures. And suddenly she felt *so* stupid in her M&M lipstick.

Nina started to go in, then she turned to Marty. "What's the matter?"

"Nothing," Marty said. "You go ahead. I'll be right there."

Nina shrugged. She tapped her lips. "Looks great," she said. "Really real." She went into the classroom.

Marty took a deep breath and counted to five. Then she walked into the room. She looked at Mr. T.'s desk. There was a pile of envelopes on it. *Pictures!* They had to be. And kids were still bringing them up, too. That must mean that they liked the idea. *Her* idea.

After a while, kids from other classes started bringing in envelopes with their pictures, too. Soon the pile got too big for Mr. T.'s desk, and they had to move it over to the table.

No one had said a word about her lipstick, except for Frank, who'd asked Marty if someone had socked her in the mouth.

At lunchtime, Mr. T. said, "Well, Ms. Gordon, I'd say, so far, this idea of yours is a resounding success."

Marty's face was hot. She knew it must be as red as her lips had been that morning. But she didn't even care. A *resounding success.*

Beverly became very busy rummaging in her desk, as if she hadn't heard Mr. Truesdale at all.

Mr. T. was getting ready to leave. "You'll need to figure out what to do with all of these, Ms. Gordon." He gestured at the pile of pictures. "But I'm sure you'll solve the problem."

Marty hooked her bangs behind her ear again and held her head very straight. She bit her bottom lip. The sweet taste was gone. She must have licked off all her lipstick without realizing it. But right then, it didn't seem that important. Mr. T. had faith in her. He thought *she* could solve the problem.

He was barely out the door, though, when Beverly started talking. "We have to get this mess organized," she said. "First, let's put the pictures in order by grade."

"Wait a minute." Nina put up her hand to stop Beverly. "I have something to say to you."

Beverly gave Nina her innocent look.

"I thought you might want to know, Miss Tattletale-Know-It-All," Nina said, "that your little plan to get me in trouble with Mr. Truesdale didn't work. In fact, he likes me now more than ever." She turned to Marty. "Doesn't he?"

Marty nodded. "He thought her drawing was a riot."

Beverly rolled her eyes. "So?" she said. "Who cares?" She fumbled with the envelopes. "Let's get started."

"Do you mind, Beverly?" Nina asked. "I mean, *do you mind?* This *is* Marty's project."

"It's the whole class's project," Beverly said. "And I *am* on the committee."

"I *said*"—Nina grabbed an envelope out of Beverly's hand—"let Marty do this."

"It's okay." Marty touched Nina's arm. "Go ahead, Beverly. Put them in order by grades."

"*Thank you.*" Beverly snatched the envelope back from Nina.

"Find the kindergartners first," Marty told Beverly. "We're going to start with them."

Beverly looked through the pile. "Here." She handed an envelope to Marty. "I'll bring out the first graders when I find them."

Marty took the envelope and went out into the hall.

Nina followed her with the tape. "Why do you let her get away with that stuff, Mart?"

Marty spread the kindergartners' pictures out on the floor and started putting them in boy-girl order. "I was going to do it that way, anyway," she said. "And it'll keep her in there—away from us."

Nina cut pieces of tape and stuck them to her chin. "But she still acts like she's in charge. And she's not. *You* are."

Marty turned toward the bulletin board so that Nina wouldn't see her smile. She was beginning to understand why Beverly liked being the boss so much. It was kind of fun.

By the end of lunch, they'd gotten only as far as the

third grade, and the bulletin board already looked crowded. Mr. T. told them to quit working until after school.

It was Nina's idea to cover the pictures on the board with a big sheet of paper to keep it a surprise until it was all done.

Then Marty and Nina hurried to the girls' room to put on more lipstick before the last bell rang.

During their silent reading period that afternoon, Mr. T. called them up, one at a time, to check the books they'd picked for their reports. When Nina was on her way back to her seat after he'd seen hers, she gave Marty the okay sign. Helen Keller must have been a hit.

Then it was Marty's turn. She gave Mr. T. her book. He flipped through it for what seemed like an age while she waited. Finally he closed the book and put it on the desk.

"Have an interest in bats, Ms. Gordon?" Mr. T. asked.

"Um . . ." Marty said. "Not—uh—*too* much."

Mr. T. tapped the book. "They're fascinating creatures. I've always been a big fan of them myself. I'll look forward to hearing what you think of this book."

She couldn't look at his eyes.

"Excellent choice," Mr. T. said. "Enjoy it."

Marty nodded. She took her book and went back to her seat.

Mr. T. loved bats. *That* was a weird thing to think about. So her bizarre little brother *wasn't* the only one. But she bet Mr. T. didn't drive everyone crazy talking about them all the time. And if *he* had a bat house, it was probably under his *own* bedroom window. Now Mr. T. thought *she* was interested in bats, too. An excellent choice, he'd said. She had Robbie to thank for that, though she'd die before she'd ever tell him. But what Mr. T. *didn't* know was that the book hadn't been Marty's choice at all. She'd just gotten stuck with it. And the worst part was, now she'd have to read it—an entire book about bats.

The rest of the afternoon dragged on. But, finally, it was three o'clock. When the dismissal bell rang, Marty and Nina and Beverly headed for the bulletin board.

"You know, I don't think he's even noticed our lipstick," Nina said to Marty.

Marty shrugged. She didn't want to tell Nina that she didn't care about it that much anymore. At least not as much as Mr. T.'s having faith in her. She cared more about that—a *lot* more.

They waited in the hall until the last kid was gone. Then Nina uncovered the board. "Ta-dah!"

Beverly had finished putting all the envelopes in order by grade, so they were stuck with her out in the hall with them.

They were taping up the pictures of Mrs. Luciano's kids when Beverly's mother came.

"I hope I'm not too late with Beverly's picture," she said. She handed Marty a manila envelope. "It wasn't ready until this afternoon."

"Oh, no," Marty said. "We haven't started on our class yet."

"Good." Mrs. Bridges stood back to look at the board.

"How nice." She smiled at Marty—one of those tight little smiles some ladies have. She turned to Beverly. "I see what you mean about the blue. But it really doesn't look *too* bad, does it?"

Nina looked like she wanted to say something to Mrs. Bridges or maybe even smack her one.

Marty was relieved when she didn't. She handed Beverly's envelope to her. "Put it with the rest of our class."

"Well, Beverly," said Mrs. Bridges, "I'll just say a quick hello to your teacher and then we'll be on our way."

"But we're not finished yet," Beverly said. "Can't I stay a little longer?"

Beverly's mother gave her a look.

"Oh"—Beverly got up from the floor and smoothed her skirt—"all right." She followed her mother into the classroom.

Marty almost felt a little sorry for Beverly. But she didn't say so. Nina would think she'd lost her mind.

As soon as Beverly and her mother were gone, Nina said, "Let me see that picture." She grabbed the envelope and tore it open. "Oh, *Mart!*"

Marty stared at the picture, hardly believing her eyes. It was big, much bigger than any of the others. And it wasn't just Beverly. It was Beverly *and* Mr. Truesdale. They were both smiling. Beverly was handing him a plant. Her mother must have taken the picture the day before school started when they came to welcome him.

"How *could* she?" Marty asked.

" 'Cause it's the kind of crummy thing Beverly does," Nina said. "And it's the kind of crummy thing her awful mother does, too." She tore off an especially long piece of tape. "I hate her mother. Don't you hate her mother?"

"Kind of." Marty looked at the bulletin board. How would she ever get the rest of the pictures on with that giant one of Beverly's to fit in?

Nina looked at her watch. "Oh, no," she said. "It's almost four o'clock. I've got to go. My cousin's coming over. You know, the one who told me about the makeup and gave me the Helen Keller book. The one who's in *seventh grade*." Nina picked up her backpack. "She'll be mad if I'm not there."

"You're *going*?" Marty had just decided that she'd have to move all the pictures down and push them even closer together to make room for their class. That could take forever.

"I've *got* to." Nina was already starting down the hall. "I'm sorry, Mart. But you're almost done." She pushed through the swinging door. "And *I* think the blue looks great."

"But, *Nina* . . ."

Marty heard the doors to the outside shut. Nina was gone.

Marty really wanted to get the board finished today. She wanted Mr. T. to know that she could do it. It had to be ready for everyone to see when they came in tomorrow morning. It just *had* to be.

Eighteen

———— ✳ ————

Marty stared at the bulletin board. Now that she'd finished putting up the pictures from Mrs. Luciano's class, there *definitely* wasn't room for Mr. T.'s. She could get maybe one row of pictures on before they'd bump into the letters at the top that said CORALWOOD FRIENDS, TOGETHER AGAIN. And her class's pictures would never fit in *one* row—especially with that giant one of Beverly's to get in.

There was room at the bottom of the board under the kindergartners, but Marty wanted *her* class to be at the top.

There was only one thing to do—move the pictures down. *All* of them. She'd have to start at the bottom with the kindergarten. Then move the first grade down, and then the second grade and keep going until she'd gotten through

Luciano's. After she'd done that, there should be enough space to fit her class at the top. There were a *lot* of pictures, though. She'd never get done in time.

Marty sighed. She took down the first kindergarten picture and moved it closer to the bottom of the board. But it wouldn't stick. It needed new tape. She cut a piece and tried to roll it into a loop to stick on the back the way that Nina had. But the tape got all bunched up in itself. She had to throw away two more pieces before she got it right. How had Nina done it so quickly?

"Ms. Gordon . . ." Mr. T. had come out into the hall. "Did the rest of the committee desert you?"

"Yeah . . . well . . ." Marty pretended to study the bulletin board. "They had to go."

"That's quite a crowd of pictures you've got up there," Mr. T. said.

"I know . . ." Marty had the most awful feeling. She was about to cry. "But there's not enough space for our class," she said. "I didn't leave room."

She hadn't planned it right. She was so stupid. And now, he'd know it.

"H-m-m-m . . ." Mr. T. took a step back.

"I have to move all the other pictures down to make enough space." Tears came into Marty's eyes, but she blinked them back.

"The janitor likes to lock up by four-thirty," Mr. T. said. "That gives you"—he looked at his watch—"just about another twenty minutes."

Twenty minutes! She'd never be able to do it in twenty minutes. Marty sighed.

"If you put your mind to it, I'll bet you can find another way," Mr. T. said, "one where you won't have to move everything."

"Well . . ." Marty said, "maybe."

With Mr. T. this close, she could hardly breathe, let alone think.

"Give it a try." Mr. T. started back to the classroom. "And holler if you need a hand."

A *hand*? What she really needed was another brain.

She looked at the board. Another way. Another way. What made him think she could find one?

There was a *lot* of room still left at the bottom of the board. If only she hadn't started the kindergartners up so high to begin with.

Then Marty had an idea. She could put some of her class's pictures across the top and some of them down the sides, kind of like a border. *If* they'd fit.

She held up David DeVoe's picture—first on one side of the board, then on the other. There was room—just enough for one row of pictures on each side.

Marty checked her watch—4:15. She dabbed her eyes with the bottom of her T-shirt. Then she made a little loop of tape for the back of David DeVoe's picture—not a bad one, either. She pressed it onto the board and picked up the next one.

She was holding the last picture—the one of Beverly, Mr. T., and the plant—when Mr. T. came out.

"Looks great," he said. "Who's getting the spot of honor in the middle there? It should go to you."

Marty showed him the picture.

"Oh, my," Mr. T. said. "Mrs. Bridges brought me a copy. But I didn't know she'd given you one for the board." He seemed a little embarrassed.

"It's a . . . a nice picture," Marty said. She wished she could cut Beverly out of it and keep the part with Mr. T. She'd sleep with his picture under her pillow every night.

"If I put it up too high, the picture covers up the letters." Marty showed him. "But if I put it too low, it covers up four of the kids in Mrs. Luciano's class."

"It *is* rather big." Mr. T. reached around Marty. "But if we slide it down behind the pictures in Mrs. Luciano's class's row, we can still see the faces and I think it will fit."

He was brilliant.

Marty took down four of the pictures from Mrs. Luciano's class and put up the picture of Beverly and Mr. T. Then she taped Mrs. Luciano's kids' pictures back up again—right over Beverly's dumb plant.

Marty took a step back from the board.

"Terrific," Mr. T. said.

It looked kind of terrific to Marty, too. The pictures weren't so crowded after all. They seemed sort of cozy, snuggled up together the way they were. And the light blue paper looked like the sky, exactly as she'd thought it would, with all the colored letters curving over it, like a real rainbow.

The janitor came down the hall, jangling his big ring of keys.

"That's the signal." Mr. T. winked at Marty. He turned to the janitor. "Just on our way out."

Marty picked up her backpack. Suddenly she felt shy standing there, alone with Mr. T.

"Wait here," he said. "I'll get my things and walk out with you. This building can seem a little spooky when it's this empty." He went back into the classroom.

Marty smoothed her T-shirt. She pulled up her socks.

Terrific. He'd said it looked terrific.

Nina would *die* when she heard about this.

Mr. Truesdale came out, carrying the brown leather bag he always had when he came in the morning. His jacket was over his arm—the navy blue one that looked so wonderful on him.

They started walking.

"You should be proud of the work you've done, Ms. Gordon," Mr. T. said. "The bulletin board looks great."

Not just good. *Great.*

Marty could smell a fantastic smell that must be his aftershave. "Thanks," she said. Her voice cracked.

She wished she could be outside herself, watching her and Mr. T. walk down the hall together—their steps matching perfectly.

Mr. T. pushed the swinging door aside and held it for her as she went through.

"Thanks." She was whispering.

When they got to the red doors that led outside, Mr. T. held the door for her again.

"Thanks," Marty said once more. She started down the steps. "Well . . ." she said, "bye . . . sir."

"Oh, Ms. Gordon, wait." Mr. T. rummaged in his leather bag. "I finished grading the class's stories. You might as well take yours with you." He handed her a paper.

It was her spelling word story—the one she'd written about the princess who rescues her brother, the prince, by filling the moat around the wicked king's palace with so much oatmeal that she is able to walk across it and bring him his magic cloak.

Marty was dying to look at it. But she didn't want Mr. T. to know how much she cared.

She folded the story in half and tucked it into the pocket of her backpack. "Thanks," she said yet again.

Then she fled down the steps.

"Good-bye, Ms. Gordon," Mr. T. called after her.

"Bye." Marty started to run, then switched to a walk—a very fast walk.

She heard the sound of what must be Mr. T.'s VW starting up. She didn't dare turn to look. Then he drove past her. He raised his hand to wave as he went by.

Marty waved, too. She watched the VW go down the street. She waited until it turned the corner. Then she tore open the pocket of her backpack and pulled out her story.

Nineteen

Marty ran all the way home. She was dying to tell someone. But the note on the kitchen table said that her mother was at a meeting. Robbie wasn't even there. He was at a friend's house. And there was no answer at Nina's.

Marty turned to the dog. "Pooh," she said, "I have wonderful news."

Pooh jumped up on Marty. His paws rested on her shoulders.

But instead of pushing him down, as she usually did, Marty held on to him and swayed as if they were dancing. "Mr. T. liked my story, Pooh," she said. "That first one *wasn't* just luck. I really *do* have a great imagination!"

Pooh struggled to get down. He broke free and ran for the back door.

Telling good news to a dog was *not* very satisfying.

Marty let Pooh out in the yard and went up to her room. But she was too excited to sit still. She picked up her bat book and flipped through it. Some of the bats in the pictures were kind of cute. Maybe the book wouldn't be so bad. After all, Mr. T. *did* think that they were fascinating creatures. But she was too fidgety to even look at pictures for very long. She closed the book and put it down on her desk.

Then she heard her mother's car pulling into the driveway. Robbie was with her. Marty could hear him yakking away as they came in the back door. She decided that if she had to tell her news with Robbie there, she might as well wait and tell the whole family together at dinner.

But it was hard to wait until then. When her mother called them to the table, Marty waited until they were all seated—her mother, her father, and Robbie. Then she waited while everyone was served. It seemed to take forever. Usually, as soon as they were settled at the table, Marty's mother asked about everyone's day. And tonight, Marty was ready for her. But Robbie started in before either of them had a chance to speak.

"Dad, can you help me put up the bat house tonight?" he asked.

"We'll see how much light is left when we've finished eating *and* the dishes are done," Mr. Gordon said.

Robbie shot a pleading look at Marty. It was his turn to load the dishwasher.

"It'll mess up the schedule," Marty said.

"Just this once . . ." Robbie said.

"Okay." Marty had been feeling more generous toward Robbie ever since he'd agreed to put the bat house up under the bathroom window instead of hers.

"Marty will do the dishes," Robbie said. "Please, Dad? *Please?*"

"I said we'll see, son." His father gave Robbie a look that shut even him right up.

Marty waited a minute more. Then she cleared her throat. "I got back another story today," she said. She tried to make it sound as if it were no big deal.

Her father, still chewing, raised his eyebrows.

"Did you bring it home?" her mother asked.

"I . . . think I have it." Marty dug in her shorts pocket and took out the paper with her story on it. She laid it on the table and smoothed its creases.

Her father took his reading glasses out of his pocket and put them on. But Marty handed the story to her mother.

Her mother looked. "Oh, Marty," she said. "This is great!"

Marty smiled. A warmth crept up her neck.

"Listen to this." Marty's mother read what Mr. T. had written. " 'Another inspired story. I love your princess!' "

Marty's ears were hot.

Her father didn't say anything. He seemed to be waiting to see for himself.

Her mother squeezed her hand. "Oh, Marty," she said again. "You must be so pleased."

124

"Can *I* see it?" Mr. Gordon asked.

"Sorry, darling." Marty's mother passed the story to him.

Robbie jumped up and stood behind, reading over his father's shoulder. Pooh got up when Robbie did. He sat at attention, his tail thumping on the floor.

Marty's father pushed his glasses up on his nose. Then he started to read and kept reading to the end. When he finally looked up, there was something like a smile on his face. "Well . . ." He turned to Marty. "This teacher of yours seems to think you have some writing talent." He handed the story to Robbie, who was still reading. "And I tend to agree with him."

Marty's own smile got wider. Her father sounded proud —of *her*. She stared at her plate and poked at her peas. She wanted to dance around the room.

"Heh-heh." Robbie was still reading. "The princess fills the moat with oatmeal." He slapped the table. "What a great way to use it."

Robbie hated oatmeal.

Marty's mother picked up her fork. "Mr. Truesdale said he loved your princess, Mart. And so do I. She's a great character. Lots of spirit, just like you."

"Yes," her father said, "like *our* princess." He smiled at Marty, and this time there was no mistaking it. It was a big, real smile.

Lots of *spirit*? That's what Nina had. Not her. Not before now.

Robbie handed Marty back her story. "I could write one

125

like that, too," he said. "But mine would be better 'cause the prince would get to do all the good stuff."

Robbie, the family brain, wanted to write a story like *hers*.

"You'd better hurry and finish," their father told Robbie, "or we won't get that bat house up tonight."

Robbie began to shovel in his food.

Marty turned to him. "Maybe I'll help you," she said. "If I get all my homework done in time." She might learn something she could use in her report.

"Really, Marth?" Robbie said. "That's great!"

"I said *maybe*."

The phone rang.

"I'll get it." Marty was already out of her chair. She dodged Pooh to get to the phone. Now she really *really* had news.

"Hello."

"Marty?"

"Oh, Nina," Marty said. "Wait till you hear this."

Twenty

———— ✳ ————

After Marty had gotten off the phone with Nina and done some of her homework, she helped Robbie with his bat house. She didn't learn anything that she could use in her report, though. Mostly, she stood next to him in the bathtub and took turns handing the hammer and nails out the window to her father on the ladder. But she did that for only a *little* while. She had other things to do—like read what Mr. T. had written on her story over and over again.

"I love your princess" is what he'd written. But if she put her finger over the *r* in the word "your," and covered up the whole word "princess," what it said was "I love you." "I love you" written in Mr. T.'s own handwriting to *her*. Marty must have read that "I love you" a zillion times. And she had it all figured out. When she was twenty-one, Mr. T.

would only be in his thirties. That wasn't such a big age difference. Maybe he'd wait for her.

On the way to school the next morning, she showed Nina what Mr. T. had written on her paper.

"Why don't you put some of that white stuff on it?" Nina asked as they came through the school yard gate. "You know, the stuff that secretaries use to cover up their mistakes? Then it would *really* look real."

"Maybe I will," Marty said. But she knew she could never bring herself to blot out even one tiny mark that Mr. T. had made.

Frank Fama was coming in the gate just as they were. "Did you finish putting up the girlie-girl bulletin board?" he asked.

"Yes." Nina stuck out her chin. "And it looks fantastic —except for *your* ugly picture."

"Yeah, well, it would look a lot better if the boys had done it," Frank said.

Nina fluffed her hair. "You *wish.*"

Then the bell rang and Frank left them behind as he ran for the door.

Nina turned to Marty. "It *does* look good, doesn't it?" she asked. "I mean, I thought the light blue was *definitely* the right choice. But after you got our class up, it didn't look *too* squished, did it?"

"I *told* you what I did." Marty yanked at the strap on her

backpack. "The way I put some of the pictures across the top and the other ones down the sides."

"Yeah . . ." Nina said, "but I just can't imagine it." She looked doubtful, very doubtful.

Sure, Mr. T. had said that it looked terrific. But what else could he say with Marty standing right there?

Marty wished she hadn't had a second bowl of cereal at breakfast. Her stomach was starting to feel kind of funny.

She and Nina climbed the stone steps and went through the big red doors. All the kids were hurrying down the hall to their classrooms. No one was paying any particular attention to Marty. But she felt as if she might as well have been wearing a big sign that said, "*I* had the idea for the bulletin board. The one with the smooshed-up pictures and the faded-looking blue paper and my dorky fourth grade picture on it."

They came to the swinging doors. Nina pushed through with her hip. She turned to see if Marty had caught it. But Marty hung back.

"*What?*" Nina asked her. "What are you *doing?*"

"I can't," Marty said. "What if it looks awful? What if they hate it?"

"Oh, come *on!*" Nina grabbed Marty's arm and pulled her through the doorway.

And there, in the hall by their room, was everybody—or nearly everybody. They were all crowded around the bulletin board. Everyone was talking and pointing and *smiling*, even the boys—just the way Marty had pictured it when she'd first had the idea.

Beverly stood by the board. "*I'm* on the committee," she said in her in-charge voice. "And *I* said, don't push. And *don't* touch the pictures."

When she saw Marty, Beverly smiled at her with a tight little smile that looked an awful lot like the one Beverly's mother had smiled yesterday.

"Hey, Bridges," a boy from Mrs. Luciano's class said. "Get a bigger picture next time, why don't you?"

"It was the only one I had," Beverly said. She turned to the board and straightened a letter that didn't need straightening.

As much as Marty hated that big picture of Beverly, she loved having Mr. T. up there. When she looked at his face, it was as if he were smiling just for her.

Then the last bell rang, and all the kids began moving toward their classrooms.

"Any student who is not in his or her seat in exactly one minute will be marked tardy!" Mrs. Luciano shouted over the sound of the bell.

Beverly leaned toward Marty. "It doesn't look as bad as I thought it would." She was almost whispering.

"Gee, thanks, Beverly."

Beverly smiled that icky smile of hers again. "You're welcome." Then she turned and went inside.

Mr. Truesdale poked his head out of the doorway. "Will

the bulletin board committee be joining us this morning?"
His smile was gorgeous.

"We'll be there in a minute," Nina said. "We just have to fix something . . . sir."

Mr. T. nodded. Then he was gone.

"Fix what?" Marty asked.

"Sh-h-h!" Nina held her finger to her lips. "Nothing. But don't you want to look at it some more?"

Marty nodded. She could have looked at that bulletin board all day.

Nina went across the hall and sat down on the floor with her back against the wall. "It looks great from over here," she said.

Marty went over and sat on the floor next to Nina. "M-m-m-m." It *did* look great. And now she knew that everyone else thought so, too. Mr. Truesdale most of all, she hoped. "I wonder if he *does* have a girlfriend," Marty said. "Maybe he doesn't." She'd been wishing that a *lot* lately.

"Nah," Nina said. "He's too cute not to have a girlfriend."

Marty shrugged. She'd decided not to tell Nina about her dream of Mr. T. waiting for her. Even though she and Nina were supposed to be a team, he could marry only one of them.

"But there's another thing . . ." Nina said.

"What?"

"I can't figure out who Mr. T.'s pet really is."

"What do you mean?"

"Well, he *loves* you," Nina said. "Obviously."

"And what about you?" Marty said. "He thinks you're funny. He even liked your joke about him in a bathing suit." She didn't mind if he *liked* Nina. You had to do more than *like* somebody to marry her.

"Yeah . . ." Nina's face got a far-off look as if she were remembering it all again.

"I think he even likes Frank," Marty said. "Do you hear the way Mr. T. laughs at his jokes?"

"Yeah." Nina pulled at the lace on her sneaker. "And they're the corniest jokes I've ever heard."

"The worst," Marty agreed. "And once I heard Mr. T. tell David DeVoe that he had an awesome aptitude for math."

"Whatever *that* is." Nina hugged her knees. "It *does* sound good, though . . . about the math."

"What about Beverly?" Marty asked. "Do you think Mr. T. knows she's a kiss-up?"

Nina nodded. "Absolutely."

"He doesn't hate her, though." Marty was positive that he'd *never* wait for Beverly.

"No-o-o . . ." Nina didn't seem to want to admit it.

"She did give him all those plants," said Marty. "And she *does* get all A's. . . ."

"So?" Nina twisted a curl around one finger. Then she untwisted it again. "What are you saying? That Mr. T. likes Beverly more than us?"

"Not *more* than us," Marty said. "It's just that maybe Mr.

132

T. doesn't play favorites. Maybe he's too cool to do that."

"So, what do you mean?" Nina said. "That we should give up our plan to be his pets? That we should just go back to being the way we used to be?"

"You mean passing notes and skipping our homework and stuff?" Marty asked. "Nah. I kind of like being the way I am, now."

"Yeah," Nina said. "Me, too. Kind of. I never had a teacher laugh at my jokes before, that's for sure."

Marty nodded. She was thinking of all the other good things, too. Like the beautiful words Mr. T. had written on her paper . . .

Nina got up. "I guess we'd better go in."

"Yeah." Marty got up, too. She tucked her bangs behind her ear. Soon they'd be long enough to stay there. She glanced at the bulletin board one more time. Then she and Nina walked into the classroom. It was going to be a wonderful year.

Make Robbie Happy,
Learn More About Bats

Dean, Anabel. *Bats, the Night Flyers*. Minneapolis, Minnesota: Lerner Publications Company, 1984.

Johnson, Sylvia. *Bats*. Minneapolis, Minnesota: Lerner Publications Company, 1985.

Novick, Alvin. *The World of Bats*. New York: Holt, Rinehart & Winston, 1969.

Pringle, Lawrence. *Batman: Exploring the World of Bats*. New York: Macmillan Publishing Company, 1991. (This is the book that Marty read for her report.)

Tuttle, Merlin. *America's Neighborhood Bats*. Austin: University of Texas Press, 1988. (Robbie got his bat house plans from this book.)

FOR MORE INFORMATION, CONTACT:
Bat Conservation International
P.O. Box 162603
Austin, Texas 78716

Educational publications and programs, books about bats, bat houses, and other bat-related items are available from this nonprofit member organization. The organization's purpose is to help people learn about the value and conservation needs of bats.